NEW LONGMAN LITERATURE

The Pearl

John Steinbeck

Text adviser: Dr Susan Shillinglaw
Director, Center for Steinbeck Studies
San José State University, California

Longman

Edinburgh Gate
Harlow, Essex

Pearson Education Limited
Edinburgh Gate
Harlow
Essex
CM20 2JE
England

First published in Great Britain in 1948
Copyright © 1945 by John Steinbeck
The right of John Steinbeck to be identified as the author of this
Work has been asserted by him in accordance with the Copyright,
Designs and Patents Act, 1988

This educational edition first published 2000
Editorial notes © Pearson Education Limited 2000

ISBN: 0582 46147 2

Printed in Singapore

The Publisher's policy is to use paper manufactured from sustainable
forests

Editorial notes by Gavin Jones
Designed and packaged by McLean Press Ltd
Cover illustration by Charlotte Combe

Contents

Introduction

About the author

John Ernst Steinbeck was born on February 27, 1902 in Salinas, California. He was the third child of John Ernst Steinbeck and Olive Hamilton Steinbeck. (Note that father and son had the same name, although the terms 'senior' and 'junior' were never used.) His father, only moderately successful in business, managed a flour mill, owned an animal feed and grain store which went bankrupt, worked for Spreckels sugar plant, and finally, when John was a teenager, found some satisfaction working as Treasurer of Monterey County. Mr Steinbeck, a keen observer of nature, taught his son to love the natural world and to accept responsibility for his own colt – an experience which is vividly recalled in the stories entitled *The Red Pony*. Steinbeck's mother, Olive, had been a schoolteacher before she married, and instilled in her son a love of books and stories. She read to him constantly – fairy tales, Stevenson's *Treasure Island*, Robin Hood stories and the Bible – all before he entered school. By the age of five he was a fluent reader himself.

At primary school, John did well. His aunt gave him an abridged copy of Sir Thomas Malory's *Le Morte d'Arthur* – later remembered by Steinbeck as the first book which was truly his own. He loved the rhythmical beat of Malory's prose, and this book stimulated his own wish to become a writer. Later in life, when already an established writer, the legends of King Arthur and the literary style of Malory were to influence much of his work.

Steinbeck's school career followed a fairly normal course. Both a little lazy and a little spoiled, John would be shy in the company of others, but he also loved playing practical jokes. He always thought of himself as a mixture of the German heritage of his father and the Irish volatility of his mother's family. Although he

1

was in advance of his classmates academically because of his mother's early influence, he became out of touch with his peers by skipping a year in the fifth grade. This meant that all through high school he was a year younger than most of his classmates.

Steinbeck decided to become a writer when he was 14 and never abandoned his dream. While in high school he began writing short stories, reading them aloud to others, and sometimes sending them, under a pseudonym, to magazines. In 1919 he graduated from high school and entered Stanford University. Here he avoided the accepted courses, attending instead classes which he thought would best help him to develop as a writer. Although he earned mostly B's in the classes he completed (with the occasional A and C grades), he withdrew from a number where he was failing.

Steinbeck never completed a degree, although he attended classes on and off for the next six years. But he enjoyed a short-story class and joined the English Club where he met other writers on the University staff – Carl Williamson, Grove Day, Carlton 'Dook' Sheffield, Margaret Bailey, Edith Mirrielees – who encouraged him to continue his writing. During summer vacations and during a year and a half break in his formal studies, he worked as a labourer in harvest fields, in a sugar-beet factory and in a laboratory. He also spent one summer at the Hopkins Marine Station in Pacific Grove – a town near Monterey where his parents had a cottage. Later, these experiences would give him material for some of his best-known novels.

Steinbeck finally dropped out of college in 1925 and went to New York City where he worked as a construction worker and later as a reporter for a newspaper – *The American*. Soon he returned to California, and went to work at a lodge and resort in the High Sierra, south of Lake Tahoe, where he started work on a novel which was eventually to appear as *Cup of Gold*. By 1928, Steinbeck had completed *Cup of Gold*, which was published in

1929. The appearance of his first full-length novel set Steinbeck on the course which was to see him produce, over the next 10 years, some of his finest work.

Steinbeck was now working on two books: *To an Unknown God* (later published as *To a God Unknown* in 1933) and another about poor farmers. In January 1930 he married Carol Henning. The couple settled in Pacific Grove. Steinbeck met Ed Ricketts, a marine biologist, who became an important influence on his writing and, subsequently, the inspiration for the fictional character Doc in the novels *Cannery Row* and *Sweet Thursday*. Steinbeck and Ricketts spent much of their time working in Ricketts' laboratory, and during their leisure hours talking about friends, neighbours, current events and relationships.

In 1932 Steinbeck hired an agent to sell his work and soon *Pastures of Heaven* was published with a contract for two more novels. The novel was enthusiastically received by the publishers Caple and Smith, but unfortunately they went bankrupt shortly afterwards. Steinbeck now had to care for his elderly parents, especially his mother who had suffered a stroke in 1933 (she died in 1934). He started writing *The Red Pony* stories by her bedside. In 1934 Steinbeck won the O. Henry Award for the best story of the year.

In 1935 *Tortilla Flat* appeared, a novel about untroubled, workshy *paisanos* who pursued a life of carefree idleness. Steinbeck based the book on his reading of the Arthurian legend, combined with a naturalistic approach suggested by his discussions with Ed Ricketts, and further developed through the stories told to him by Susan Gregory, a local Spanish teacher, who spent much of her time amongst the local community of Spanish-speaking workers. The book was an immediate success, becoming a best seller and bringing Steinbeck, and the town of Monterey, to the notice of a wider public. In 1936 Steinbeck produced *In Dubious Battle*, a book about Labour organisers which caused controversy from both the left and the right of the political spectrum, some claiming that the strike leaders were portrayed as being too ruthless, while others said that Steinbeck showed too much sympathy towards communists. However, the effect of this argument was that Steinbeck's name was now firmly in the mind of the American public. *Of Mice and Men*, one of his most poignant books, was published in 1937. The story of George and Lennie, two itinerant farm labourers, was cast as a play in novel form. It became a best seller and was chosen by the Book-of-the-Month Club. Steinbeck also rewrote it as a play which opened on Broadway in November 1937 directed by George S. Kaufman. This production won the Drama Critics Circle Award for 1937.

It was at this time that Steinbeck was asked by the chief editor of the *San Francisco News* to write a series of articles on farmers who had migrated to California from the Southwest dustbowl. He toured the camps in the San Joaquin Valley where he was shocked by the squalor and filth of the squatters' camps in contrast with the clean and well-organised government settlements. At this time also, he met Tom Collins, a camp manager and sympathiser with the migrant workers, who campaigned tirelessly to improve the poor conditions in the camps. Steinbeck's experiences on this trip formed the basis for what many regard as his greatest work – *The Grapes of Wrath*. His acknowledgement of Collins' help and contribution appears in the second part of the novel's dedication, 'To Tom, Who Lived It'.

The manuscript was finished in late 1938 and at Carol's suggestion was given the title *The Grapes of Wrath* (taken from The Battle Hymn of the Republic). The book was published in early 1939 and was soon in the best-seller list where it remained well into the next year, finally establishing Steinbeck as a major serious novelist. *The Grapes of Wrath* won attention not only as a literary work but also as a political statement, but some readers declared it to be deliberately and exaggeratedly shocking until Eleanor Roosevelt, wife of the American President, toured some of the migrant camps and declared Steinbeck's portrayal of them to be accurate.

Exhausted after completing this epic novel, Steinbeck turned to other projects, first making a documentary film in Hollywood, and then working with Ed Ricketts in the field of marine biology. In 1940 the Steinbecks joined Ed Ricketts on a marine research trip to the Gulf of California, the literary outcome of which was *Sea of Cortez*, co-authored by Ricketts. It was on this trip also that Steinbeck first heard the story of a boy and a giant pearl which he later recast as the short novel *The Pearl*. On returning to California, the Steinbecks learned that *The Grapes of Wrath* had been awarded the Pulitzer Prize. His marriage to Carol had become increasingly tense, and in 1943 they divorced. Shortly after, Steinbeck married Gwendolyn Conger.

During the early 1940s, Steinbeck was deeply involved in the war effort as an unpaid consultant for various government propaganda agencies and for the US Air Force. In 1942, *The Moon is Down* was published, a story about the invasion of a neutral country based closely on the German invasion of Norway. It was another immediate success for Steinbeck, even outselling *The Grapes of Wrath*. Like *Of Mice and Men*, Steinbeck had written the novel in play form, and once again a stage version appeared a few months later. He also wrote scripts for propaganda films, most notably in his work on *Bombs Away* and Alfred Hitchcock's *Lifeboat*. In 1943 he was sent to London as a reporter for the New York *Herald Tribune*, later moving with troops of the American Army Air Force to North Africa, where he covered the invasion of Italy. Some of the articles he filed during this period were later collected in a book *Once There Was a War*, published in 1958.

Steinbeck and Gwyn moved back to Monterey in 1944 and

Cannery Row appeared in 1945. The story centres on the character Doc, who is closely modelled on Ed Ricketts, and incorporates many of the types that Steinbeck and Ricketts had met and studied years before. But Steinbeck found that 'you can't go home again', so he and Gwyn moved back to New York City with Thom, their first son, who was born in 1944. *The Pearl* and *The Wayward Bus* both appeared in 1947.

In 1948, Ed Ricketts was killed when his car was hit by a train. Steinbeck was devastated by the death of his close friend and mentor. His marriage to Gwyn was also becomingly increasingly unstable, and Steinbeck returned from a short trip to Mexico to find that Gwyn had returned to her family in Los Angeles, taking their sons Thom and John with her. Soon after, they divorced. Steinbeck was devastated and spent the next year back in Pacific Grove.

In 1950 he married Elaine Scott, former wife of film star Zachary Scott. They settled in New York and Steinbeck started work on his 'big book' which was to be a gift to his sons to teach them about their heritage. Telling the story of two families and spanning the period from the American Civil War to the end of the Great War, *East of Eden* was published in 1952. It sold well but some critics expected Steinbeck to have produced yet another book in the tradition of *Of Mice and Men* and could not appreciate the breadth of this new venture. After six months' extensive travel in Europe, the Steinbecks returned to New York City and bought a property at Sag Harbour on Long Island for summers and weekends, where Steinbeck spent his time writing while Elaine was left to look after his two sons by Gwyn Conger (who spent the summers with him) as well as her own daughter, Waverly. *Sweet Thursday* – a revision of *Cannery Row* – appeared in 1954 to mixed reviews, and after yet another critical attack on his humorous novel *The Short Reign of Pippin IV* in 1957, Steinbeck embarked on a modern language version of Malory's *Le Morte d'Arthur* (the first book he loved), a project which he never completed.

The Winter of Our Discontent, a semi-autobiographical account of a small-town shopkeeper, Ethan Hawley, who ends up with the hopes and emotions of a successful writer, was published in 1961. The author's life in Sag Harbour, and his feelings about his children and his relationship with them, provided much of the material for this book. *The Winter of Our Discontent* proved to be Steinbeck's last major work of fiction.

In 1962 Steinbeck published *Travels with Charley in Search of America*, a record of a journey he made in a custom-built motor caravan with Elaine's large poodle, Charley. In the same year he achieved his greatest honour when he was awarded the Nobel Prize for Literature. Although he was one of only six American writers who had achieved this honour, the award was deemed controversial by a section of the American press.

In 1967 Steinbeck, whose elder son was involved in the war, went to Vietnam as a reporter for *Newsday*, but soon realised that he could not give his unquestioning support to the war effort, although he continued to back the soldiers in their thankless task. On his return to the United States in April 1967, Steinbeck was operated on for a back injury. After some months of ill health, John Steinbeck died of heart failure in December 1968 and is buried in Salinas, California.

Setting the scene

In 1940 John Steinbeck, his wife Carol and their friend Ed Ricketts made a research trip to the Gulf of California. Taking a break from the work of collecting and identifying specimens of marine life, they visited La Paz. It was here that Steinbeck first heard the tale of a boy and a giant pearl which became the inspiration for this short novel, published in 1947. In his youth, Steinbeck had frequently encountered Mexican immigrant workers in his home town of Salinas and later in Monterey. He had worked with them on farms and in factories and felt that he understood them, their concerns and interests. He must have listened to their stories on many occasions and developed a style of writing which closely mirrored their simple way of telling their tales – with scattered references to family and friends, to gods and devils, and to the natural world around them.

In the preface to a collected edition of his short novels, Steinbeck wrote of *The Pearl*, 'I tried to write it as folklore, to give it that set-aside, raised-up feeling that all folk stories have.' In so doing, Steinbeck has altered the original tale considerably, but has also given it a timeless quality. The narrative style is descended directly from the great traditions of the Anglo-Saxon epic *Beowulf*, Chaucer's *Canterbury Tales* and Malory's *Le Morte d'Arthur*, and retains a flavour of the spoken word – we can visualise ourselves sitting as Steinbeck may have sat, listening intently to a local story-teller; we hear his voice, we even imagine that we are listening to and understanding Spanish, so skilled is Steinbeck at transferring the idiom and cadences of that language into the English of the simple field and factory workers he knew so well.

Summary of the plot
The Pearl tells the story of Kino, a young pearl fisherman who lives in a native village on the outskirts of the town of La Paz on the shores of the Gulf of California. Kino has a wife and a newborn baby, both of whom he adores. One day, Kino finds an immense pearl of superb quality. Immediately, he sees a bright future for his family. As the news of Kino's luck spreads, others try to benefit from it: a greedy doctor, pretending to save the life of the baby who has been bitten by a scorpion, tries to bargain for the pearl; thieves try to steal it at night; crooked dealers try to cheat him of

its true value. Even the beggars hope to benefit 'for they knew that there is no alms-giver in the world like a poor man who is suddenly lucky'. One night Kino kills a man who tries to rob him. Later, Kino's hut is burned down and in fear for their lives, Kino and his wife, Juana, decide to run away to another town in the north. However, they are followed, and in a desperate attempt to save himself and his family, Kino kills the three pursuers. In the struggle, the baby is killed. Kino and Juana return to their village and throw the pearl back into the sea.

Main characters

The story centres on Kino and his struggle against evil. Kino seems to be different from the other villagers in that he has strong feelings about his life and the people close to him which he expresses as songs in his head – perhaps Steinbeck is trying to tell the reader that Kino, more than others in his village, has a powerful imagination. Kino's determination to better himself and his family with the proceeds of the giant pearl is probably quite surprising to his fellows, who cannot imagine a future without struggle. Kino finds it difficult to put his thoughts into words, and when his brother, Juan Tomás, asks him what he will do now he is rich, Kino's answers come fitfully and almost as if he cannot believe what he is actually saying. He instinctively understands the power of education when he announces that Coyotito will go to school, but cannot resist the need to express his own manhood symbolically – 'A rifle,' he said. 'Perhaps a rifle.' After the customs of the village, Kino and Juana are man and wife, but Kino shows his awareness of the status of a church wedding and of outward appearances: 'We will be married – in the church.' And later: 'We will have new clothes.'

When his courage and ingenuity falter, Kino is supported by his partner, Juana. She shares the work while acknowledging Kino's authority. Steinbeck says of her, 'In the canoe she was like a strong man', and 'She could stand hunger and fatigue almost better than Kino himself.' But we are also told that she is 'obedient and respectful.' Yet it is Juana who shows herself to be as revolutionary in her thinking as Kino when she insists that he fetch the European doctor from the town to tend Coyotito's scorpion sting. During the pursuit, when Kino proposes leading the trackers astray so that Juana and Coyotito can escape, Juana is adamant that they must stick together.

Steinbeck gives other characters in *The Pearl* less substance. The most rounded are the European doctor and the pearl buyer. The doctor is consumed with dissatisfaction and greed. His outward appearance and manner is gentle and soft, which disguises his true nature. The beggars outside the church 'knew his ignorance, his cruelty, his avarice, his appetites, his sins … They had seen his corpses go into the church.' We first see him trying to live in a style which he imagines is truly French, and therefore in his opinion, civilised. He hates La Paz and the 'little Indians' and longs to escape. Such is his ambition that he will even make Coyotito ill so that he can 'cure' him and have a chance to gain the pearl.

The pearl buyer whom Kino visits appears to be a kindly man. 'His face was fatherly and benign' we are told, 'He was … a jolly man who knew all jokes' but who could also 'remember the death of your aunt' and appear to grieve for your loss. He is, in fact, a consummate actor who can control his audience, but who is himself controlled by his fear of his shadowy employer. His nervousness is measured by the manner in which he practises legerdemain with a coin – trickery comes naturally to him.

The priest, although also of European extraction and more motivated by money than the natives, has lesser ambitions. His thoughts on hearing about the pearl turn to church repairs, and later to whether Kino and Juana have been 'properly' married or whether Coyotito has been baptised. Like the doctor, he is compelled by the news of the pearl to make the effort to visit Kino in the Indian village, but he maintains his dignity and contents himself with an indirect approach: 'I hope thou wilt remember to give thanks, my son, to Him who has given thee this treasure, and to pray for guidance in the future.' The message is quite clear to Kino.

The other inhabitants of the Indian village are represented by Kino's elder brother, Juan Tomás and his wife Apolonia. It is Juan Tomás who asks Kino about his plans for the future, thus satisfying the curiosity of the whole village. He also acts as a support and a go-between when Kino is in trouble – but Kino is not entirely sure whether he can trust his brother and promises to leave as soon as possible, recognising also, perhaps, that Apolonia will never be able to keep the secret of his whereabouts for long.

Main themes

There is a strong moral theme in *The Pearl*. We understand that this incredible gift can be used for either good or evil. Kino sees the pearl as his passport to a better life: a harpoon for himself or even a rifle; education for his baby son, Coyotito; a real wedding in a church; new and fancy clothes for Juana. As a procession of people visit his brush hut in an attempt to register a claim on his new-found wealth, Kino becomes increasingly defensive, eventually retreating into almost animal behaviour in guarding his treasure. The news of the pearl also sets other men afire with greed, leading them to attempt to steal it at the risk of their lives. Eventually, Kino is driven to kill in order to save himself and his family from certain death. The pearl claims one final victim in the person of Coyotito, the baby, before Kino is finally persuaded to abandon his hopes for the future and to follow Juana's advice and return the pearl to the sea.

Steinbeck also seems to dwell with some pessimism on the idea that we cannot escape from our destinies, and that if we try we will be punished. Kino's attempt to use the pearl to free himself

11

and his family from the poverty and depression of life in the Indian village results in the deaths of several people, culminating in that of Coyotito – a terrible punishment for one who believes in the importance of sons.

Language and style

The Pearl is a simple tale of the struggle between good and evil. Steinbeck chose to cast the story as an allegory – claiming that all such stories are told and retold until the finer details are lost and all that is left are good things and bad things – black and white with no shades in between. It is ironic that the forces of evil are not represented, as one might have expected, by the mysteries and superstitions of the native Mexicans in their village of brushwood huts, but rather by the apparently civilized European conquerors who live in the stone and plaster town of La Paz. These are the ones who try to cheat Kino of his pearl and who are prepared to kill for it – who, on hearing the news of his discovery, can only think how they can benefit from it: the doctor who longs to return to the Paris of his youth; the priest who suddenly remembers that Kino and Juana have not been married in his church; the dealers who see this as a way to win reward from their employer.

Steinbeck makes much use of musical images in The Pearl, giving each of Kino's emotions an imaginary song. There is the unsung Song of the Family, which can be one of contentment or on occasion a fierce call to defence. The pearl has its own song, which is triumphant and misleads Kino into thinking he can defeat the evil which comes with it. Other 'songs' are attached to Evil and Enemies. When the villagers silently watch Kino and Juana returning childless to the village, Kino's Song of the Family 'was as fierce as a cry. He was immune and terrible, and his song had become a battle cry'. Steinbeck tells us that Kino's ancestors had been great song makers, but that now all the songs were old ones – there were no new songs. Kino's expression of his feelings in secret songs may indicate that he has retained some of the ancient quality of imagination. It may be just this imagination which at first leads him into great danger and later enables him to overcome the tragic loss of his child and eventually even become a respected member of the village once more. In 1945, Steinbeck wrote about recording the music for a film of *The Pearl* which was being made in Mexico: 'Gwyn (Steinbeck's second wife) made some recordings of the basic music – the Family and Pearl themes. The Evil music is not finished...'. He goes on to say that 'these themes are ancient Indian music long preceding the conquest. And I think they are beautiful.' It would seem from these extracts that Steinbeck felt that the music of the Native Mexicans was inextricably bound up with their culture, and so he made Kino think and feel in musical terms.

Steinbeck was continually experimenting with the form of his novels. *Of Mice and Men* and *The Moon is Down* were both conceived as incorporating elements of both plays and novels. In *The Pearl*, Steinbeck turned instead to the idea of a film-novel. Many of the scenes are intensely visual and minutely described. They could be said to add little to the actual narrative, but serve a vital purpose in creating parallels to the main action and in fixing a mood or atmosphere. The detailed description of the pools where Kino and Juana are finally brought to bay is an instance of this filmic technique which Steinbeck uses as a feature in the novel by emphasising the presence of both life and death by the pools.

The Pearl is in a tradition used by storytellers for centuries – that of using folk tale styles and techniques to make a moral point. Such tales never seem to lose their impact, even when every detail of them is intimately known to the reader or listener. It is up to future readers of this story to judge how successful Steinbeck has been in emulating the work of such writers as Chaucer, Malory, the brothers Grimm and Hans Christian Andersen.

The Pearl

'In the town they tell the story of the great pearl – how it was found how it was lost again. They tell of Kino, the fisherman, and of his wife, Juana, and of the baby, Coyotito. And because the story has been told so often, it has taken root in every man's mind. And, as with all retold tales that are in people's hearts, there are only good and bad things and black and white things and good and evil things and no in-between anywhere.

If this story is a parable, perhaps everyone takes his own meaning from it and reads his own life into it. In any case, they say in the town that …'

Notes for Chapter 1

Kino and his wife Juana live with their baby Coyotito (little coyote) in a brushwood hut on the shores of the Gulf of California. They are native Mexicans, and their village is on the edge of a Spanish Mexican town. Dawn is breaking. They rise, eat a simple breakfast and tend the baby. There is a feeling of contentment until they see a scorpion crawling towards the baby. Kino tries to kill the scorpion but it falls on the baby and stings it. Juana insists that they visit the doctor in the town.

What do you think?
As you read this first chapter, think about how Kino's feelings and emotions are expressed:
- in terms of music and song
- through his senses
- by physical action.

Questions
Look for evidence in Chapter 1 to help you answer these questions.
1. In what ways does Steinbeck show the depth of feeling between Kino and Juana?
2. Why do you think that no new songs were being added to the old songs of Kino's people?
3. How does Steinbeck show Kino's awareness and understanding of animals?
4. In what way does Juana's behaviour surprise Kino when the scorpion stings Coyotito?
5. The doctor's servant 'shut the gate quickly out of shame.' (page 28). Why do you think the servant felt shame?

Further activity
John Steinbeck first heard the story of the Pearl of the World in a village near La Paz when he was on a scientific expedition in the Gulf of California. Find out where the Gulf of California and La Paz are and as much as you can about the area including scenery, climate, population, language, employment etc. Prepare an article suitable for a guidebook to the area. Draw a map and include the places which are mentioned in the story as you come across them.

Chapter 1

Kino awakened in the near dark. The stars still shone and the day had drawn only a pale wash of light in the lower sky to the east. The roosters had been crowing for some time, and the early pigs were already beginning their ceaseless turning of twigs and bits of wood to see whether anything to eat had been overlooked. Outside the brush house in the tuna clump, a covey of little birds chittered and flurried with their wings.

Kino's eyes opened, and he looked first at the lightening square which was the door and then he looked at the hanging box where Coyotito slept. And last he turned his head to Juana, his wife, who lay beside him on the mat, her blue head-shawl over her nose and over her breasts and around the small of her back. Juana's eyes were open too. Kino could never remember seeing them closed when he awakened. Her dark eyes made little reflected stars. She was looking at him as she was always looking at him when he awakened.

Kino heard the little splash of morning waves on the beach. It was very good – Kino closed his eyes again to listen to his music. Perhaps he alone did this and perhaps all of his people did it. His people had once been great makers of songs so that everything they saw or thought or did or heard became a song. That was very long ago. The songs remained; Kino knew them, but no new songs were added. That does not mean that there were no personal songs. In Kino's head there was a song now, clear and soft, and if he had been able to speak of it, he would have called it the Song of the Family.

His blanket was over his nose to protect him from the dank air. His eyes flicked to a rustle beside him. It was Juana arising, almost soundlessly. On her hard bare feet she went to the hanging box where Coyotito slept, and she leaned over and said a little reassuring word. Coyotito looked up for a moment, and closed his eyes and slept again.

Juana went to the fire pit and uncovered a coal and fanned it alive while she broke little pieces of brush over it.

Now Kino got up and wrapped his blanket about his head and nose and shoulders. He slipped his feet into his sandals and went outside to watch the dawn.

Outside the door he squatted down and gathered the blanket ends about his knees. He saw the specks of Gulf clouds flame high in the air. And a goat came near and sniffed at him and stared with its cold yellow eyes. Behind him Juana's fire leaped into flame and threw spears of light through the chinks of the brush house wall and threw a wavering square of light out the door. A late moth blustered in to find the fire. The Song of the Family came now from behind Kino. And the rhythm of the family song was the grinding-stone where Juana worked the corn for the morning cakes.

The dawn came quickly now, a wash, a glow, a lightness, and then an explosion of fire as the sun arose out of the Gulf. Kino looked down to cover his eyes from the glare. He could hear the pat of the corn-cakes in the house and the rich smell of them on the cooking plate. The ants were busy on the ground, big black ones with shiny bodies, and little dusty quick ants. Kino watched with the detachment of God while a dusty ant frantically tried to escape the sand trap an ant lion had dug for him. A thin, timid dog came close and, at a soft word from Kino, curled up, arranged its tail nearly over its feet, and laid its chin delicately on the pile. It was a black dog with yellow-gold spots where its eyebrows should have been. It was a morning like other mornings and yet perfect among mornings.

Kino heard the creak of the rope when Juana took Coyotito out of his hanging box and cleaned him and hammocked him in her shawl in a loop that placed him close to her breast. Kino could see these things without looking at them. Juana sang softly an ancient song that had only three notes and yet endless variety of interval. And this was part of the family song too. It was all part. Sometimes it rose to an aching chord that caught the throat, saying this is safety, this is warmth, this is the *Whole*.

Across the brush fence were other brush houses, and the smoke came from them too, and the sound of breakfast, but those were other songs, their pigs were other pigs, their wives were not Juana. Kino was young and strong and his black hair hung over his brown forehead. His eyes were warm and fierce and bright and his moustache was thin and coarse. He lowered his blanket from his nose now, for the dark poisonous air was gone and the yellow sunlight fell on the house. Near the brush fence two roosters bowed and feinted at each other with squared wings and neck feathers ruffed out. It would be a clumsy fight. They were not game chickens. Kino watched them for a moment, and then his eyes went up to a flight of wild doves twinkling inland to the hills. The world was awake now, and Kino arose and went into his brush house.

As he came through the door Juana stood up from the glowing fire pit. She put Coyotito back in his hanging box and then she combed her black hair and braided it in two braids and tied the ends with thin green ribbon. Kino squatted by the fire pit and rolled a hot corn-cake and dipped it in sauce and ate it, and he drank a little pulque; and that was breakfast. That was the only breakfast he had ever known outside of feast days and one incredible fiesta on cookies that had nearly killed him. When Kino had finished, Juana came back to the fire and ate her breakfast. They had spoken once, but there is not need for speech if it is only a habit anyway. Kino sighed with satisfaction – and that was conversation.

The sun was warming the brush house, breaking through its crevices in long streaks. And one of the streaks fell on the hanging box where Coyotito lay, and on the ropes that held it.

It was a tiny movement that drew their eyes to the hanging box. Kino and Juana froze in their positions.

Down the rope that hung the baby's box from the roof support a scorpion moved slowly. His stinging tail was straight out behind him, but he could whip it up in a flash of time.

Kino's breath whistled in his nostrils and he opened his mouth to stop it. And then the startled look was gone from him and the rigidity from his body. In his mind a new song had come, the Song of Evil, the music of the enemy, of any foe of the family, a savage, secret, dangerous melody, and, underneath, the Song of the Family cried plaintively.

The scorpion moved delicately down the rope towards the box. Under her breath Juana repeated an ancient magic to guard against such evil, and on top of that she muttered a Hail Mary between clenched teeth. But Kino was in motion. His body glided quietly across the room, noiselessly and smoothly. His hands were in front of him, palms down, and his eyes were on the scorpion. Beneath it in the hanging box Coyotito laughed and reached up his hand towards it. It sensed danger when Kino was almost within reach of it. It stopped, and its tail rose up over its back in little jerks and the curved thorn on the tail's end glistened.

Kino stood perfectly still. He could hear Juana whispering the old magic again, and he could hear the evil music of the enemy. He could not move until the scorpion moved, and it felt for the source of the death that was coming to it. Kino's hand went forward very slowly, very smoothly. The thorned tail jerked upright. And at that moment the laughing Coyotito shook the rope and the scorpion fell.

Kino's hand leaped to catch it, but it fell past his fingers, fell on the baby's shoulder, landed and struck. Then, snarling, Kino had it, had it in his fingers, rubbing it to a paste in his hands. He threw it down and beat it into the earth floor with his fist, and Coyotito screamed with pain in his box. But Kino beat and stamped the enemy until it was only a fragment and a moist place in the dirt. His teeth were bared and fury flared in his eyes and the Song of the Enemy roared in his ears.

But Juana had the baby in her arms now. She found the puncture with redness starting from it already. She put her lips down over the puncture and sucked hard and spat and sucked again while Coyotito screamed.

Kino hovered; he was helpless, he was in the way.

The screams of the baby brought the neighbours. Out of their brush houses they poured – Kino's brother Juan Tomás and his fat wife Apolonia and their four children crowded in the door and blocked the entrance, while behind them others tried to look in, and one small boy crawled among legs to have a look. And those in front passed the word back to those behind – 'Scorpion. The baby has been stung.'

Juana stopped sucking the puncture for a moment. The little hole was slightly enlarged and its edges whitened from the sucking, but the red swelling extended farther around it in a hard lymphatic mound. And all of these people knew about the scorpion. An adult might be very

22

ill from the sting, but a baby could easily die from the poison. First, they knew, would come swelling and fever and tightened throat, and then cramps in the stomach, and then Coyotito might die if enough of the poison had gone in. But the stinging pain of the bite was going away. Coyotito's screams turned to moans.

Kino had wondered often at the iron in his patient, fragile wife. She, who was obedient and respectful and cheerful and patient, could arch her back in child pain with hardly a cry. She could stand fatigue and hunger almost better than Kino himself. In the canoe she was like a strong man. And now she did a most surprising thing.

'The doctor,' she said. 'Go to get the doctor.'

The word was passed out among the neighbours where they stood close-packed in the little yard behind the brush fence. And they repeated among themselves, 'Juana wants the doctor.' A wonderful thing, a memorable thing, to want the doctor. To get him would be a remarkable thing. The doctor never came to the cluster of brush houses. Why should he, when he had more than he could do to take care of the rich people who lived in the stone and plaster houses of the town?

'He would not come,' the people in the yard said.

'He would not come,' the people in the door said, and the thought got into Kino.

'The doctor would not come,' Kino said to Juana.

She looked up at him, her eyes as cold as the eyes of a lioness. This was Juana's first baby – this was nearly

23

everything there was in Juana's world. And Kino saw her determination and the music of the family sounded in his head with a steely tone.

'Then we will go to him,' Juana said, and with one hand she arranged her dark-blue shawl over her head and made of one end of it a sling to hold the moaning baby and made of the other end of it a shade over his eyes to protect him from the light. The people in the door pushed against those behind to let her through. Kino followed her. They went out of the gate to the rutted path and the neighbours followed them.

The thing had become a neighbourhood affair. They made a quick soft-footed procession into the centre of the town, first Juana and Kino, and behind them Juan Tomás and Apolonia, her big stomach jiggling with the strenuous pace, then all the neighbours with the children trotting on the flanks. And the yellow sun threw their black shadows ahead of them so that they walked on their own shadows.

They came to the place where the brush houses stopped and the city of stone and plaster began, the city of harsh outer walls and inner cool gardens where a little water played and the bougainvillaea crusted the walls with purple and brick-red and white. They heard from the secret gardens the singing of caged birds and heard the splash of cooling water on hot flagstones. The procession crossed the blinding plaza and passed in front of the church. It had grown now, and on the outskirts the hurrying newcomers were being softly informed how the baby had been stung by a scorpion, how the father and mother were taking it to the doctor.

And the newcomers, particularly the beggars from the front of the church, who were great experts in financial analysis, looked quickly at Juana's old blue skirt, saw the tears in her shawl, appraised the green ribbon on her braids, read the age of Kino's blanket and the thousand washings of his clothes, and set them down as poverty people and went along to see what kind of drama might develop. The four beggars in front of the church knew everything in the town. They were students of the expressions of young women as they went in to confession, and they saw them as they came out and read the nature of the sin. They knew every little scandal and some very big crimes. They slept at their posts in the shadow of the church so that no one crept in for consolation without their knowledge. And they knew the doctor. They knew his ignorance, his cruelty, his avarice, his appetites, his sins. They knew his clumsy abortions and the little brown pennies he gave sparingly for alms. They had seen his corpses go into the church. And, since early mass was over and business was slow, they followed the procession, these endless searchers after perfect knowledge of their fellow men, to see what the fat lazy doctor would do about an indigent baby with a scorpion bite.

The scurrying procession came at last to the big gate in the wall of the doctor's house. They could hear the splashing water and the singing of caged birds and the sweep of the long brooms on the flagstones. And they could smell the frying of good bacon from the doctor's house.

Kino hesitated a moment. This doctor was not of his people. This doctor was of a race which for nearly four hundred years had beaten and starved and robbed and despised Kino's race, and frightened it too, so that the indigene came humbly to the door. And, as always when he came near to one of this race, Kino felt weak and afraid and angry at the same time. Rage and terror went together. He could kill the doctor more easily than he could talk to him, for all of the doctor's race spoke to all of Kino's race as though they were simple animals. And as Kino raised his right hand to the iron ring knocker in the gate, rage swelled in him, and the pounding music of the enemy beat in his ears, and his lips drew tight against his teeth – but with his left hand he reached to take off his hat. The iron ring pounded against the gate. Kino took off his hat and stood waiting. Coyotito moaned a little in Juana's arms, and she spoke softly to him. The procession crowded close, the better to see and hear.

After a moment the big gate opened a few inches. Kino could see the green coolness of the garden and little splashing fountain through the opening. The man who looked out at him was one of his own race. Kino spoke to him in the old language. 'The little one – the first-born – has been poisoned by the scorpion,' Kino said. 'He requires the skill of the healer.'

The gate closed a little, and the servant refused to speak

in the old language. 'A little moment,' he said. 'I go to inform myself,' and he closed the gate and slid the bolt home. The glaring sun threw the bunched shadows of the people blackly on the white wall.

In his chamber the doctor sat up in his high bed. He had on his dressing-gown of red watered silk that had come from Paris, a little tight over the chest now if it was buttoned. On his lap was a silver tray with a silver chocolate pot and a tiny cup of egg-shell china, so delicate that it looked silly when he lifted it with his big hand, lifted it with the tips of thumb and forefinger and spread the other three fingers wide to get them out of the way. His eyes rested in puffy little hammocks of flesh and his mouth drooped with discontent. He was growing very stout, and his voice was hoarse with the fat that pressed on his throat. Beside him on a table was a small Oriental gong and a bowl of cigarettes. The furnishings of the room were heavy and dark and gloomy. The pictures were religious, even the large tinted photograph of his dead wife, who, if masses willed and paid for out of her own estate could do it, was in Heaven. The doctor had once for a short time been a part of the great world and his whole subsequent life was memory and longing for France. 'That,' he said, 'was civilised living' – by which he meant that on a small income he had been able to keep a mistress and eat in restaurants. He poured his second cup of chocolate and crumbled a sweet biscuit in his fingers. The servant from the gate came to the open door and stood waiting to be noticed.

'Yes?' the doctor asked.

'It is a little Indian with a baby. He says a scorpion stung it.'

The doctor put his cup down gently before he let his anger rise.

'Have I nothing better to do than cure insect bites for "little Indians"? I am a doctor, not a veterinary.'

'Yes, Patron,' said the servant.

'Has he any money?' the doctor demanded. 'No, they never have any money. I, I alone in the world am supposed to work for nothing – and I am tired of it. See if he has any money!'

At the gate the servant opened the door a trifle and looked out at the waiting people. And this time he spoke in the old language.

'Have you money to pay for the treatment?'

Now Kino reached into a secret place somewhere under his blanket. He brought out a paper folded many times. Crease by crease he unfolded it, until at last there came to view eight small misshapen seed pearls, as ugly and grey as little ulcers, flattened and almost valueless. The servant took the paper and closed the gate again, but this time he was not gone long. He opened the gate just wide enough to pass the paper back.

'The doctor has gone out,' he said. 'He was called to a serious case.' And he shut the gate quickly out of shame.

And now a wave of shame went over the whole procession. They melted away. The beggars went back to the church steps, the stragglers moved off, and the neighbours departed so that the public shaming of Kino would not be in their eyes.

For a long time Kino stood in front of the gate with Juana beside him. Slowly he put his suppliant hat on his head. Then, without warning, he struck the gate a crushing blow with his fist. He looked down in wonder at his split knuckles and at the blood that flowed down between his fingers.

Notes for Chapter 2

After their rejection by the doctor, Kino and Juana go out pearl fishing. On his first dive Kino finds a massive oyster. He returns with his catch to the canoe. He opens the giant oyster and finds a huge pearl inside it. Juana notices that Coyotito's scorpion sting has faded.

What do you think?
As you read this chapter, think how Steinbeck uses words and images connected with light to describe:
- the scenery of the estuary
- appearance of the sea bed
- Kino's eyes when he returns to the canoe
- the first sight of the great pearl.

Questions
1. How does Steinbeck's description of the life under the sea differ from that of life on land?
2. Steinbeck makes a connection between the description of Kino's canoe and the formation of pearls. What is this connection and why do you think he makes it?
3. Why does Juana have no faith in her method of treating Coyotito's injury?
4. Why is Kino unwilling to open the great oyster?
5. Why does Kino howl when Juana points out what has happened to Coyotito?

Further activity
Although Kino and Juana do not feel the need to talk very often, finding the pearl is such an important event that Kino will be certain to tell Juana every detail of what his feelings were as he started his dive and when he saw the great oyster. Write two or three paragraphs in which Kino tells Juana how he found the great oyster and what feelings he experienced. Try to use the kind of language and imagery that Steinbeck might have used if he were to have written such a section in his book. Working with a partner, make a tape recording of your description in which you take the part of Kino, adding suitable background music or similar sound effects.

Chapter 2

The town lay on a broad estuary, its old yellow plastered buildings hugging the beach. And on the beach the white and blue canoes that came from Nayarit were drawn up, canoes preserved for generations by a hard shell-like waterproof plaster whose making was a secret of the fishing people. They were high and graceful canoes with curving bow and stern and a braced section midships where a mast could be stepped to carry a small lateen sail.

The beach was yellow sand, but at the water's edge a rubble of shell and algæ took its place. Fiddler crabs bubbled and sputtered in their holes in the sand, and in the shallows little lobsters popped in and out of their tiny homes in the rubble and sand. The sea bottom was rich with crawling and swimming and growing things. The brown algæ waved in the gentle currents and the green eel-grass swayed and little sea horses clung to its stems. Spotted botete, the poison fish, lay on the bottom in the eel-grass beds, and the bright-coloured swimming crabs scampered over them.

On the beach the hungry dogs and the hungry pigs of the town searched endlessly for any dead fish or sea bird that might have floated in on a rising tide.

Although the morning was young, the hazy mirage was up. The uncertain air that magnified some things and blotted out others hung over the whole Gulf so that all sights were unreal and vision could not be trusted; so that sea and land had the sharp clarities and the vagueness of a dream. Thus it might be that the people of the Gulf trust things of the spirit and things of the imagination, but they do not trust their eyes to show them distance or clear outline or any optical exactness. Across the estuary from the town one section of mangroves stood clear and telescopically defined, while another mangrove clump was a hazy black-green blob. Part of the far shore disappeared into a shimmer that looked like water. There was no certainty in seeing, no proof that what you saw was there or was not there. And the people of the Gulf expected all places were that way, and it was not strange to them. A copper haze hung over the water, and the hot morning sun beat on it and made it vibrate blindingly.

The brush houses of the fishing people were back from the beach on the right-hand side of the town, and the canoes were drawn up in front of this area.

Kino and Juana came slowly down to the beach and to Kino's canoe, which was the one thing of value he owned in the world. It was very old. Kino's grandfather had brought it from Nayarit, and he had given it to Kino's father, and so it had come to Kino. It was at once property and source of food, for a man with a boat can guarantee a woman that she will eat something. It is the bulwark against starvation. And every year Kino refinished his canoe with the hard shell-like plaster by the secret method that had also come to him from his father. Now he came to the canoe and touched the bow tenderly as he always did. He laid his diving rock and his basket and the two ropes in the sand by the canoe. And he folded his blanket and laid it in the bow.

Juana laid Coyotito on the blanket, and she placed her shawl over him so that the hot sun could not shine on him. He was quiet now, but the swelling on his shoulder had continued up his neck and under his ear and his face was puffed and feverish. Juana went to the water and waded in. She gathered some brown seaweed and made a flat damp poultice of it, and this she applied to the baby's swollen shoulder, which was as good a remedy as any and probably better than the doctor could have done. But the remedy lacked his authority because it was simple and didn't cost anything. The stomach cramps had not come to Coyotito. Perhaps Juana had sucked out the poison in time, but she had not sucked out her worry over her first-born. She had not prayed directly for the recovery of the baby – she had prayed that they might find a pearl with which to hire the doctor to cure the baby, for the minds of people are as unsubstantial as the mirage of the Gulf.

Now Kino and Juana slid the canoe down the beach to the water, and when the bow floated, Juana climbed in, while Kino pushed the stern in and waded beside it until it floated lightly and trembled on the little breaking waves. Then in co-ordination Juana and Kino drove their double-bladed paddles into the sea, and the canoe creased the water and hissed with speed. The other pearlers were gone out long since. In a few moments Kino could see them clustered in the haze, riding over the oyster bed.

Light filtered down through the water to the bed where the frilly pearl oysters lay fastened to the rubbly bottom, a bottom strewn with shells of broken, opened oysters. This was the bed that had raised the King of Spain to be a great power in Europe in past years, had helped to pay for his wars, and had decorated the churches for his soul's sake. The grey oysters with ruffles like skirts on the shells, the barnacle-crusted oysters with little bits of weed clinging to the skirts and small crabs climbing over them. An accident could happen to these oysters, a grain of sand could lie in the folds of muscle and irritate the flesh until in self-protection the flesh coated the grain with a layer of smooth cement. But once started, the flesh continued to coat the foreign body until it fell free in some tidal flurry or until the oyster was destroyed. For centuries men had dived down and torn the oysters from their beds and ripped them open, looking for the coated grains of sand. Swarms of fish lived near the bed to live near the oysters thrown back by the searching men and to nibble at the shining inner shells. But the pearls were accidents, and the finding of one was luck, a little pat on the back by God or the gods or both.

Kino had two ropes, one tied to a heavy stone and one to a basket. He stripped off his shirt and trousers and laid his hat in the bottom of the canoe. The water was oily smooth. He took his rock in one hand and his basket in the other, and he slipped feet-first over the side and the rock carried him to the bottom. The bubbles rose behind him until the water cleared and he could see. Above, the surface of the water was an undulating mirror of brightness, and he could see the bottoms of the canoes sticking through it.

Kino moved cautiously so that the water would not be obscured with mud or sand. He hooked his foot in the loop on his rock and his hands worked quickly, tearing the oysters loose, some singly, others in clusters. He laid them in his basket. In some places the oysters clung to one another so that they came free in lumps.

Now, Kino's people had sung of everything that happened or existed. They had made songs to the fishes, to the sea in anger and to the sea in calm, to the light and the dark and the sun and the moon, and the songs were all in Kino and in his people – every song that had ever been made, even the ones forgotten. And as he filled his basket the song was in Kino, and the beat of the song was his pounding heart as it ate the oxygen from his held breath, and the melody of the song was the grey-green water and the little scuffling animals and the clouds of fish that flitted by and were gone. But in the song there was a secret little inner song, hardly perceptible, but always there, sweet and secret and clinging, almost hiding in the counter-melody, and this was the Song of the Pearl That Might Be, for every shell thrown in the basket might contain a pearl. Chance was against it, but luck and the gods might be for it. And in the canoe above him Kino knew that Juana was making the magic of prayer, her face set rigid and her muscles hard to force the luck, to tear the luck out of the gods' hands, for she needed the luck for the swollen shoulder of Coyotito. And because the need was great and the desire was great, the little secret melody of the pearl that might be was stronger this morning. Whole phrases of it came clearly and softly into the Song of the Undersea.

Kino, in his pride and youth and strength, could remain down over two minutes without strain, so that he worked deliberately, selecting the largest shells. Because they were disturbed, the oyster shells were tightly closed. A little to his right a hummock of rubbly rock struck up, covered with young oysters not ready to take. Kino moved next to the hummock, and then, beside it, under a little overhang, he saw a very large oyster lying by itself, not covered with its clinging brothers. The shell was partly open, for the overhang protected this ancient oyster, and in the lip-like muscle Kino saw a ghostly gleam, and then the shell closed down. His heart beat out a heavy rhythm and the melody of the maybe pearl shrilled in his ears. Slowly he forced the oyster loose and held it tightly against his breast. He kicked his foot free from the rock loop, and his body rose to the surface and his black hair gleamed in the sunlight. He reached over the side of the canoe and laid the oyster in the bottom.

Then Juana steadied the boat while he climbed in. His eyes were shining with excitement, but in decency he pulled up his rock, and then he pulled up his basket of oysters and lifted them in. Juana sensed his excitement, and she pretended to look away. It is not good to want a thing too much. It sometimes drives the luck away. You must want it just enough, and you must be very tactful with God or the gods. But Juana stopped breathing. Very deliberately Kino opened his short strong knife. He looked speculatively at the basket. Perhaps it would be better to open *the* oyster last. He took a small oyster from the basket, cut the muscle, searched the folds of flesh, and threw it in the water. Then he seemed to see the great oyster for the first time. He squatted in the bottom of the canoe, picked up the shell and examined it. The flutes were shining black to brown, and only a few small barnacles adhered to the shell. Now Kino was reluctant to open it. What he had seen, he knew, might be a reflection, a piece of flat shell accidentally drifted in or a complete illusion. In this Gulf of uncertain light there were more illusions than realities.

But Juana's eyes were on him and she could not wait. She put her hand on Coyotito's covered head. 'Open it,' she said softly.

Kino deftly slipped his knife into the edge of the shell. Through the knife he could feel the muscle tighten hard. He worked the blade lever-wise and the closing muscle and the shell fell apart. The lip-like flesh writhed up and then subsided. Kino lifted the flesh, and there it lay, the great pearl, perfect as the moon. It captured the light and refined it and gave it back in silver incandescence. It was as large as a seagull's egg. It was the greatest pearl in the world.

Juana caught her breath and moaned a little. And to Kino the secret melody of the maybe pearl broke clear and beautiful, rich and warm and lovely, glowing and gloating and triumphant. In the surface of the great pearl he could see dream forms. He picked the pearl from the dying flesh and held it in his palm, and he turned it over and saw that its curve was perfect. Juana came near to stare at it in his hand, and it was the hand he had smashed against the doctor's gate, and the torn flesh of the knuckles was turned greyish white by the sea water.

Instinctively Juana went to Coyotito where he lay on his father's blanket. She lifted the poultice of seaweed and looked at the shoulder. 'Kino,' she cried shrilly.

He looked past his pearl, and he saw that the swelling was going out of the baby's shoulder, the poison was receding from its body. Then Kino's fist closed over the pearl and his emotion broke over him. He put back his head and howled. His eyes rolled up and he screamed and his body was rigid. The men in the other canoes looked up, startled, and then they dug their paddles into the sea and raced towards Kino's canoe.

Notes for Chapter 3

News of Kino's pearl spreads, evoking different responses. Kino visits his brother and wife to seek advice, and makes plans for the future. The priest arrives, followed by the doctor who had earlier refused to treat Coyotito. Kino hides the pearl, but in the night, a thief tries to find it, and Kino is hurt while defending his property.

What do you think?
Most of those who hear of Kino's good fortune only think of how it can benefit them. Think how their reactions differ. Think also how Steinbeck describes these reactions as being like a poison, like the scorpion's venom which infected Coyotito.

Questions
1. What does Steinbeck mean when he describes the town as 'a colonial animal'?
2. How are we made to realise how little concern for the natives the Spanish Mexican inhabitants of the town have?
3. How do we know that Kino is suspicious of both the priest and the doctor?
4. Why do you think that Steinbeck chooses this point in his story to describe the behaviour of the schools of fish in the estuary?
5. Both Kino and Juana realise that in some way the pearl will bring evil to them. How do their opinions differ about the best way to turn away this evil?

Further activity
Now that you have met a number of the main characters, start a characterlog. For each character, draw up a chart in four columns headed *Key Point*, *Comment*, *Quotation* and *Page*. In the first column include details of appearance, what the character says or has said about him or her, what s/he does and any other evidence which may help to build up a picture of the character. In the second column make brief notes about what the information in Column 1 tells you about the character. Write appropriate quotations in the third column to support what you have put in the first two columns. Give a page reference in the fourth column so you can check back – e.g. when revising.

Chapter 3

A town is a thing like a colonial animal. A town has a nervous system and a head and shoulders and feet. A town is a thing separate from all other towns, so that there are no two towns alike. And a town has a whole emotion. How news travels through a town is a mystery not easily to be solved. News seems to move faster than small boys can scramble and dart to tell it, faster than women can call it over the fences.

Before Kino and Juana and the other fishers had come to Kino's brush house, the nerves of the town were pulsing and vibrating with the news – Kino had found the Pearl of the World. Before panting little boys could strangle out the words, their mothers knew it. The news swept on past the brush houses, and it washed in a foaming wave into the town of stone and plaster. It came to the priest walking in his garden, and it put a thoughtful look in his eyes and a memory of certain repairs necessary to the church. He wondered what the pearl would be worth. And he wondered whether he had baptized Kino's baby, or married him for that matter. The news came to the shopkeepers, and they looked at men's clothes that had not sold so well.

The news came to the doctor where he sat with a woman whose illness was age, though neither she nor the doctor would admit it. And when it was made plain who Kino was, the doctor grew stern and judicious at the same time. 'He is a client of mine,' the doctor said. 'I am treating his child for a scorpion sting.' And the doctor's eyes rolled up a little in their fat hammocks and he thought of Paris. He remembered the room he had lived in there as a great and luxurious place, and he remembered the hard-faced woman who had lived with him as a beautiful and kind girl, although she had been none of these three. The doctor looked past his aged patient and saw himself sitting in a restaurant in Paris and a waiter was just opening a bottle of wine.

The news came early to the beggars in front of the church, and it made them giggle a little with pleasure, for they knew that there is no alms-giver in the world like a poor man who is suddenly lucky.

Kino had found the Pearl of the World. In the town, in little offices, sat the men who bought pearls from the fishers. They waited in their chairs until the pearls came in, and then they cackled and fought and shouted and threatened until they reached the lowest price the fisherman would stand. But there was a price below which they dared not go, for it had happened that a fisherman in despair had given his pearls to the church. And when the buying was over, these buyers sat alone and their fingers played restlessly with the pearls, and they wished they owned the pearls. For there were not many buyers really – there was only one, and he kept these agents in separate offices to give a semblance of competition. The news came to these men, and their eyes squinted and their finger-tips burned a little, and each one thought how the patron could not live for ever and someone had to take his place. And each one thought how with some capital he could get a new start.

All manner of people grew interested in Kino – people with things to sell and people with favours to ask. Kino had found the Pearl of the World. The essence of pearl mixed with essence of men and a curious dark residue was precipitated. Every man suddenly became related to Kino's pearl, and Kino's pearl went into the dreams, the speculations, the schemes, the plans, the futures, the wishes, the needs, the lusts, the hungers, of everyone, and only one person stood in the way and that was Kino, so that he became curiously every man's enemy. The news stirred up something infinitely black and evil in the town; the black distillate was like a scorpion, or like hunger in the smell of food, or like loneliness when love is withheld. The poison sacs of the town began to manufacture venom, and the town swelled and puffed with the pressure of it.

But Kino and Juana did not know these things. Because they were happy and excited they thought everyone shared their joy. Juan Tomás and Apolonia did, and they were the world too. In the afternoon, when the sun had gone over the mountains of the Peninsula to sink in the outward sea, Kino squatted in his house with Juana beside him. And the brush house was crowded with neighbours. Kino held the great pearl in his hand, and it was warm and alive in his hand. And the music of the pearl had merged with the music of the family so that one beautified the other. The neighbours looked at the pearl in

Kino's hand and they wondered how such luck could come to any man.

And Juan Tomás, who squatted on Kino's right hand because he was his brother, asked, 'What will you do now that you have become a rich man?'

Kino looked into his pearl, and Juana cast her eyelashes down and arranged her shawl to cover her face so that her excitement could not be seen. And in the incandescence of the pearl the pictures formed of the things Kino's mind had considered in the past and had given up as impossible.

In the pearl he saw Juana and Coyotito and himself standing and kneeling at the high altar, and they were being married now that they could pay. He spoke softly:

'We will be married – in the church.'

In the pearl he saw how they were dressed – Juana in a shawl stiff with newness and a new skin, and from under the long skirt Kino could see that she wore shoes. It was in the pearl – the picture glowing there. He himself was dressed in new white clothes, and he carried a new hat – not of straw but of fine black felt – and he too wore shoes – not sandals but shoes that laced. But Coyotito – he was the one – he wore a blue sailor suit from the United States and a little yachting cap such as Kino had seen once when a pleasure-boat put into the estuary. All of these things Kino saw in the lucent pearl, and he said, 'We will have new clothes.'

And the music of the pearl rose like a chorus of trumpets in his ears.

Then to the lovely grey surface of the pearl came the little things Kino wanted: a harpoon to take the place of one lost a year ago, a new harpoon of iron with a ring in the end of the shaft; and – his mind could hardly make the leap – a rifle – but why not, since he was so rich? And Kino saw Kino in the pearl, Kino holding a Winchester carbine. It was the wildest day-dreaming and very pleasant. His lips moved hesitantly over this – 'A rifle,' he said. 'Perhaps a rifle.'

It was the rifle that broke down the barriers. This was an impossibility, and if he could think of having a rifle whole horizons were burst and he could rush on. For it is said that humans are never satisfied, that you give them one thing and they want something more. And this is said in disparagement, whereas it is one of the greatest talents the species has and one that has made it superior to animals that are satisfied with what they have.

The neighbours, close pressed and silent in the house, nodded their heads at his wild imaginings. And a man in the rear murmured, 'A rifle. He will have a rifle.'

But the music of the pearl was shrilling with triumph in Kino. Juana looked up, and her eyes were wide at Kino's courage and at his imagination. And electric strength had come to him now the horizons were kicked out. In the pearl he saw Coyotito sitting at a little desk in school, just as Kino had once seen it through an open door. And Coyotito was dressed in a jacket, and he had on a white collar and a broad silken tie. Moreover, Coyotito was writing on a big piece of paper. Kino looked at his neighbours fiercely. 'My son will go to school,' he said, and the neighbours were hushed. Juana caught her breath sharply. Her eyes were bright as she watched him, and she looked quickly down at Coyotito in her arms to see whether this might be possible.

But Kino's face shone with prophecy. 'My son will read and open the books, and my son will write and will know writing. And my son will make numbers, and these things will make us free because he will know – he will know and through him we will know.' And in the pearl Kino saw himself and Juana squatting by the little fire in the brush hut while Coyotito read from a great book. 'This is what the pearl will do,' said Kino. And he had never said so many words together in his life. And suddenly he was afraid of his talking. His hand closed down over the pearl and cut the light away from it. Kino was afraid as a man is afraid who says, 'I will,' without knowing.

Now the neighbours knew they had witnessed a great marvel. They knew that time would now date from Kino's pearl, and that they would discuss this moment for many years to come. If these things came to pass, they would recount how Kino looked and what he said and how his eyes shone, and they would say, 'He was a man transfigured. Some power was given to him, and there it started. You see what a great man he has become, starting from that moment. And I myself saw it.'

And if Kino's planning came to nothing, those same neighbours would say, 'There it started. A foolish madness came over him so that he spoke foolish words.

God keep us from such things. Yes, God punished Kino because he rebelled against the way things are. You see what has become of him. And I myself saw the moment when his reason left him.'

Kino looked down at his closed hand and the knuckles were scabbed over and tight where he had struck the gate.

Now the dusk was coming. And Juana looped her shawl under the baby so that he hung against her hip, and she went to the fire hole and dug a coal from the ashes and broke a few twigs over it and fanned a flame alive. The little flames danced on the faces of the neighbours. They knew they should go to their own dinners, but they were reluctant to leave.

The dark was almost in, and Juana's fire threw shadows on the brush walls when the whisper came in, passed from mouth to mouth: 'The Father is coming – the priest is coming.' Then men uncovered their heads and stepped back from the door, and the women gathered their shawls about their faces and cast down their eyes. Kino and Juan Tomás, his brother, stood up. The priest came in – a greying, ageing man with an old skin and a young sharp eye. Children he considered these people, and he treated them like children.

'Kino,' he said softly, 'thou art named after a great man and a great Father of the Church.' He made it sound like a benediction. 'Thy namesake tamed the desert and sweetened the minds of thy people, didst thou know that? It is in the books.'

Kino looked quickly down at Coyotito's head, where he

47

hung on Juana's hip. Some day, his mind said, that boy would know what things were in the books and what things were not. The music had gone out of Kino's head, but now, thinly, slowly, the melody of the morning, the music of evil, of the enemy, sounded, but it was faint and weak. And Kino looked at his neighbours to see who might have brought this song in.

But the priest was speaking again. 'It has come to me that thou hast found a great fortune, a great pearl.'

Kino opened his hand and held it out, and the priest gasped a little at the size and beauty of the pearl. And then he said, 'I hope thou wilt remember to give thanks, my son, to Him who has given thee this treasure, and to pray for guidance in the future.'

Kino nodded dumbly, and it was Juana who spoke softly. 'We will, Father. And we will be married now. Kino has said so.' She looked at the neighbours for confirmation, and they nodded their heads solemnly.

The priest said, 'It is pleasant to see that your first thoughts are good thoughts. God bless you, my children.' He turned and left quietly, and the people let him through.

But Kino's hand had closed tightly on the pearl again, and he was glancing about suspiciously, for the evil song was in his ears, shrilling against the music of the pearl.

The neighbours slipped away to go to their houses, and Juana squatted by the fire and set her clay pot of boiled beans over the little flame. Kino stepped to the doorway and looked out. As always, he could smell the smoke from many fires, and he could see the hazy stars and feel the damp of the night air, so that he covered his nose from it. The thin dog came to him and threshed itself in greeting like a wind-blown flag, and Kino looked down at it and didn't see it. He had broken through the horizons into a cold and lonely outside. He felt alone and unprotected, and scraping crickets and shrilling tree frogs and croaking toads seemed to be carrying the melody of evil. Kino shivered a little and drew his blanket more tightly against his nose. He carried the pearl still in his hand, tightly closed in his palm, and it was warm and smooth against his skin.

Behind him he heard Juana patting the cakes before she put them down on the clay cooking-sheet. Kino felt all the warmth and security of his family behind him, and the Song of the Family came from behind him like the purring of a kitten. But now, by saying what his future was going to be like, he had created it. A plan is a real thing, and things projected are experienced. A plan once made and visualised becomes a reality along with other realities – never to be destroyed but easily to be attacked. Thus Kino's future was real, but having set it up, other forces were set up to destroy it, and this he knew, so that he had to prepare to meet the attack. And this Kino knew also – that the gods do not love men's plans, and the gods do not love success unless it comes by accident. He knew that the gods take their revenge on a man if he be successful through his own efforts. Consequently Kino was afraid of plans, but, having made one, he could never destroy it.

And to meet the attack, Kino was already making a hard skin for himself against the world. His eyes and his mind probed for danger before it appeared.

Standing in the door, he saw two men approach; and one of them carried a lantern which lighted the ground and the legs of the men. They turned in through the opening of Kino's brush fence and came to his door. And Kino saw that one was the doctor and the other the servant who had opened the gate in the morning. The split knuckles on Kino's right hand burned when he saw who they were.

The doctor said, 'I was not in when you came this morning. But now, at the first chance, I have come to see the baby.'

Kino stood in the door, filling it, and hatred raged and flamed in the back of his eyes, and fear too, for the hundreds of years of subjugation were cut deep in him.

'The baby is nearly well now,' he said curtly.

The doctor smiled, but his eyes in their little lymph-lined hammocks did not smile.

He said, 'Sometimes, my friend, the scorpion sting has a curious effect. There will be apparent improvement, and then without warning – pouf!' He pursed his lips and made a little explosion to show how quick it could be, and he shifted his small black doctor's bag about so that the light of the lamp fell upon it, for he knew that Kino's race love the tools of any craft and trust them. 'Sometimes,' the doctor went on in a liquid tone, 'sometimes there will be a withered leg or a blind eye or a crumpled back. Oh, I

50

know the sting of the scorpion, my friend, and I can cure it.'

Kino felt the rage and hatred melting towards fear. He did not know, and perhaps the doctor did. And he could not take the chance of putting his certain ignorance against this man's possible knowledge. He was trapped as his people were always trapped, and would be until, as he had said, they could be sure that the things in the books were really in the books. He could not take a chance – not with the life or with the straightness of Coyotito. He stood aside and let the doctor and his man enter the brush hut.

Juana stood up from the fire and backed away as he entered, and she covered the baby's face with the fringe of her shawl. And when the doctor went to her and held out his hand, she clutched the baby tight and looked at Kino where he stood with the fire shadows leaping on his face.

Kino nodded, and only then did she let the doctor take the baby.

'Hold the light,' the doctor said, and when the servant held the lantern high, the doctor looked for a moment at the wound on the baby's shoulder. He was thoughtful for a moment and then he rolled back the baby's eyelid and looked at the eyeball. He nodded his head while Coyotito struggled against him.

'It is as I thought,' he said. 'The poison has gone inwards and it will strike soon. Come, look!' He held the eyelid down. 'See – it is blue.' And Kino, looking anxiously, saw that indeed it was a little blue. And he didn't know whether or not it was always a little blue. But the trap was set. He couldn't take the chance.

The doctor's eyes watered in their little hammocks. 'I will give him something to try to turn the poison aside,' he said. And he handed the baby to Kino.

Then from his bag he took a little bottle of white powder and a capsule of gelatine. He filled the capsule with the powder and closed it, and then around the first capsule he fitted a second capsule and closed it. Then he worked very deftly. He took the baby and pinched its lower lip until it opened its mouth. His fat fingers placed the capsule far back on the baby's tongue, beyond the point where he could spit it out, and then from the floor he picked up the little pitcher of pulque and gave Coyotito a drink, and it was done. He looked again at the baby's eyeball and he pursed his lips and seemed to think.

At last he handed the baby back to Juana, and he turned to Kino. 'I think the poison will attack within the hour,' he said. 'The medicine may save the baby from hurt, but I will come back in an hour. Perhaps I am in time to save him.' He took a deep breath and went out of the hut, and his servant followed him with the lantern.

Now Juana had the baby under her shawl, and she stared at it with anxiety and fear. Kino came to her, and he lifted the shawl and stared at the baby. He moved his hand to look under the eyelid, and only then saw that the pearl was still in his hand. Then he went to a box by the wall, and from it he brought a piece of rag. He wrapped the pearl in the rag, then went to the corner of the brush house and dug a little hole with his fingers in. the dirt floor, and he put the pearl in the hole and covered it up and concealed the place. And then he went to the fire, where Juana was squatting, watching the baby's face.

The doctor, back in his house, settled into his chair and looked at his watch. His people brought him a little supper of chocolate and sweet cakes and fruit, and he stared at the food discontentedly.

In the houses of the neighbours the subject that would lead all conversations for a long time to come was aired for the first time to see how it would go. The neighbours showed one another with their thumbs how big the pearl was, and they made little caressing gestures to show how lovely it was. From now on they would watch Kino and Juana very closely to see whether riches turned their heads, as riches turn all people's heads. Everyone knew why the doctor had come. He was not good at dissembling and he was very well understood.

Out in the estuary a tight-woven school of small fishes glittered and broke water to escape a school of great fishes that drove in to eat them. And in the houses the people could hear the swish of the small ones and the bouncing splash of the great ones as the slaughter went on. The dampness arose out of the Gulf and was deposited on bushes and cacti and on little trees in salty drops. And the night mice crept about on the ground and the little night hawks hunted them silently.

The skinny black puppy with flame spots over his eyes came to Kino's door and looked in. He nearly shook his hind quarters loose when Kino glanced up at him, and he subsided when Kino looked away. The puppy did not enter the house, but he watched with frantic interest while Kino ate his beans from the little pottery dish and wiped it clean with a corn-cake and ate the cake and washed the whole down with a drink of pulque.

Kino was finished and was rolling a cigarette when Juana spoke sharply. 'Kino.' He glanced at her and then got up and went quickly to her, for he saw fright in her eyes. He stood over her, looking down, but the light was very dim. He kicked a pile of twigs into the fire hole to make a blaze, and then he could see the face of Coyotito. The baby's face was flushed and his throat was working and a little thick drool of saliva issued from his lips. The spasm of the stomach muscles began, and the baby was very sick.

Kino knelt beside his wife. 'So the doctor knew,' he said, but he said it for himself as well as for his wife, for his mind was hard and suspicious and he was remembering the white powder. Juana rocked from side to side and moaned out the little Song of the Family as though it could ward off the danger, and the baby vomited and writhed in her arms. Now uncertainty was in Kino, and the music of evil throbbed in his head and nearly drove out Juana's song.

The doctor finished his chocolate and nibbled the little fallen pieces of sweet cake. He brushed his fingers on a napkin, looked at his watch, arose, and took up his little bag.

The news of the baby's illness travelled quickly among the brush houses, for sickness is second only to hunger as the enemy of poor people. And some said softly, 'Luck, you see, brings bitter friends.' And they nodded and got up to go to Kino's house. The neighbours scuffled with covered noses through the dark until they crowded into Kino's house again. They stood and gazed, and they made little comments on the sadness that this should happen at a time of joy, and they said, 'All things are in God's hands.' The old women squatted down beside Juana to try to give her aid if they could and comfort if they could not.

Then the doctor hurried in, followed by his man. He scattered the old women like chickens. He took the baby and examined it and felt its head. 'The poison it has worked,' he said. 'I think I can defeat it. I will try my best.' He asked for water, and in the cup of it he put three drops of ammonia, and he prised open the baby's mouth and poured it down. The baby spluttered and screeched under the treatment, and Juana watched him with haunted eyes. The doctor spoke a little as he worked. 'It is lucky that I know about the poison of the scorpion, otherwise –'and he shrugged to show what could have happened.

But Kino was suspicious, and he could not take his eyes from the doctor's open bag, and from the bottle of white powder there. Gradually the spasms subsided and the baby relaxed under the doctor's hands. And then Coyotito sighed deeply and went to sleep, for he was very tired with vomiting.

The doctor put the baby in Juana's arms. 'He will get well now,' he said. 'I have won the fight.' And Juana looked at him with adoration.

The doctor was closing his bag now. He said, 'When do you think you can pay this bill?' He said it even kindly.

'When I have sold my pearl I will pay you,' Kino said.

'You have a pearl? A good pearl?' the doctor asked with interest.

And then the chorus of the neighbours broke in. 'He has found the Pearl of the World,' they cried, and they joined forefinger with thumb to show how great the pearl was.

'Kino will be a rich man,' they clamoured. 'It is a pearl such as one has never seen.'

The doctor looked surprised. 'I had not heard of it. Do you keep this pearl in a safe place? Perhaps you would like me to put it in my safe?'

Kino's eyes were hooded now, his cheeks were drawn taut. 'I have it secure,' he said. 'Tomorrow I will sell it and then I will pay you.'

The doctor shrugged, and his wet eyes never left Kino's eyes. He knew the pearl would be buried in the house, and he thought Kino might look towards the place where it was buried. 'It would be a shame to have it stolen before you could sell it,' the doctor said, and he saw Kino's eyes flick involuntarily to the floor near the side post of the brush house.

When the doctor had gone and all the neighbours had reluctantly returned to their house Kino squatted beside the little glowing coals in the fire hole and listened to the night sound, the soft sweep of the little waves on the shore and the distant barking of dogs, the creeping of the breeze through the brush house roof and the soft speech of his neighbours in their houses in the village. For these people do not sleep soundly all night; they awaken at intervals and talk a little and then go to sleep again. And after a while Kino got up and went to the door of his house.

He smelled the breeze and he listened for any foreign sound of secrecy or creeping, and his eyes searched the darkness, for the music of evil was sounding in his head and he was fierce and afraid. After he had probed the night with his senses he went to the place by the side post where the pearl was buried, and he dug it up and brought it to his sleeping-mat, and under his sleeping-mat he dug another little hole in the dirt floor and buried his pearl and covered it up again.

And Juana, sitting by the fire hole, watched him with questioning eyes, and when he had buried his pearl she asked, 'Who do you fear?'

Kino searched for a true answer, and at last he said, 'Everyone.' And he could feel a shell of hardness drawing over him.

After a while they lay down together on the sleeping-mat, and Juana did not put the baby in his box to-night, but cradled him on her arms and covered his face with her shawl. And the last light went out of the embers in the fire hole.

But Kino's brain burned, even during his sleep, and he

dreamed that Coyotito could read, that one of his own people could tell him the truth of things. And in his dream, Coyotito was reading from a book as large as a house, with letters as big as dogs, and the words galloped and played on the book. And then darkness spread over the page, and with the darkness came the music of evil again, and Kino stirred in his sleep; and when he stirred, Juana's eyes opened in the darkness. And then Kino awakened, with the evil music pulsing in him, and he lay in the darkness with his ears alert.

Then from the corner of the house came a sound so soft that it might have been simply a thought, a little furtive movement, a touch of a foot on earth, the almost inaudible purr of controlled breathing. Kino held his breath to listen, and he knew that whatever dark thing was in his house was holding its breath too, to listen. For a time no sound at all came from the corner of the brush house. Then Kino might have thought he had imagined the sound. But Juana's hand came creeping over to him in warning, and then the sound came again! – the whisper of a foot on dry earth and the scratch of fingers in the soil.

And now a wild fear surged in Kino's breast, and on the fear came rage, as it always did. Kino's hand crept into his breast where his knife hung on a string, and then he sprang like an angry cat, leaped striking and spitting, for the dark thing he knew was in the corner of the house. He felt cloth, struck at it with his knife and missed, and struck again and felt his knife go through cloth, and then his head crashed with lightning and exploded with pain.

There was a soft scurry in the doorway, and running steps for a moment, and then silence.

Kino could feel warm blood running down from his forehead, and he could hear Juana calling to him, 'Kino! Kino!' And there was terror in her voice. Then coldness came over him as quickly as the rage had, and he said, 'I am all right. The thing has gone.'

He groped his way back to the sleeping-mat. Already Juana was working at the fire. She uncovered an ember from the ashes and shredded little pieces of corn-husk over it and blew a little flame into the corn-husks so that a tiny light danced through the hut. And then from a secret place Juana brought a little piece of consecrated candle and lighted it at the flame and set it upright on a fireplace stone. She worked quickly, crooning as she moved about. She dipped the end of her head-shawl in water and swabbed the blood from Kino's bruised forehead. 'It is nothing,' Kino said, but his eyes and his voice were hard and cold and a brooding hate was growing in him.

Now the tension which had been growing in Juana boiled up to the surface and her lips were thin. 'This thing is evil,' she cried harshly. 'This pearl is like a sin! It will destroy us,' and her voice rose shrilly. 'Throw it away, Kino. Let us break it between stones. Let us bury it and forget the place. Let us throw it back into the sea. It has brought evil. Kino, my husband, it will destroy us.' And in the firelight her lips and her eyes were alive with her fear.

But Kino's face was set, and his mind and his will were set. 'This is our one chance,' he said. 'Our son must go to school. He must break out of the pot that holds us in.'

'It will destroy us all,' Juana cried. 'Even our son.'

'Hush,' said Kino. 'Do not speak any more. In the morning we will sell the pearl, and then the evil will be gone, and only the good remain. Now hush, my wife.' His dark eyes scowled into the little fire, and for the first time he knew that his knife was still in his hands, and he raised the blade and looked at it and saw a little line of blood on the steel. For a moment he seemed about to wipe the blade on his trousers, but then he plunged the knife into the earth and so cleansed it.

The distant roosters began to crow and the air changed and the dawn was coming. The wind of the morning ruffled the water of the estuary and whispered through the mangroves, and the little waves beat on the rubbly beach with an increased tempo. Kino raised the sleeping-mat and dug up his pearl and put it in front of him and stared at it.

And the beauty of the pearl, winking and glimmering in the light of the little candle, cozened his brain with its beauty. So lovely it was, so soft, and its own music came from it – its music of promise and delight, its guarantee of the future, of comfort, of security. Its warm lucence promised a poultice against illness and a wall against insult. It closed a door on hunger. And as he stared at it Kino's eyes softened and his face relaxed. He could see the little image of the consecrated candle reflected in the soft surface of the pearl, and he heard again in his ears the lovely music of the undersea, the tone of the diffused green light of the sea bottom. Juana, glancing secretly at him, saw him smile. And because they were in some way one thing and one purpose, she smiled with him.

And they began this day with hope.

Notes for Chapter 4

The following morning Kino, Juana and Coyotito, followed by a great crowd, walk into the town to sell the pearl. To his fury, the buyers will only offer a small amount, claiming that the pearl has little value. Kino returns to his hut and hides the pearl. As dusk falls he senses evil around him. When he steps outside he is attacked and searched. He and Juana decide to travel to the capital to find a buyer for the pearl.

What do you think?
The villagers sense that they are witnessing a great event. Notice how Steinbeck shows the variety of excuses in their minds for joining the procession into town. Think about how the support of the villagers for Kino and Juana fades as they come to believe the dealers' lies.

Questions
1. Why do the pearl fishers still go to the dealers even though they know they are being cheated by them?
2. What do you think is the priest's real intention in the sermon that Kino refers to on page 68?
3. How do the 'dramatic effects' (see page 71) of the dealer and Kino differ?
4. Why is Juan Tomás afraid for Kino (page 67)?
5. What does Kino mean when he tells Juana, 'Believe me, I am a man,' and what is Juana's answer to this?

Further activity
We know that all the pearl buyers are employed by the same man. They are also frightened of him. Imagine that you are the buyer who failed to persuade Kino to part with his pearl for 1,000 pesos. Your employer will want to know why you failed. Write a letter reporting what your preparations were for cheating Kino, how these plans failed and what further steps you intend to take to get hold of the pearl. Remember that you are afraid of your employer and will probably wish to place the blame for your failure on somebody else. Write your letter in the sort of language the dealer might have used, judging by his manner as described on pages 73–74.

Chapter 4

It is wonderful the way a little town keeps track of itself and of all its units. If every single man and woman, child and baby, acts and conducts itself in a known pattern and breaks no walls and differs with no one and experiments in no way and is not sick and does not endanger the ease and peace of mind or steady unbroken flow of the town, then that unit can disappear and never be heard of. But let one man step out of the regular thought or the known and trusted pattern, and the nerves of the townspeople ring with nervousness and communication travels over the nerve lines of the town. Then every unit communicates to the whole.

Thus, in La Paz, it was known in the early morning through the whole town that Kino was going to sell his pearl that day. It was known among the neighbours in the brush huts, among the pearl fishermen; it was known among the Chinese grocery-store owners; it was known in the church, for the altar boys whispered about it. Word of it crept in among the nuns; the beggars in front of the church spoke of it, for they would be there to take the tithe of the first-fruits of the luck. The little boys knew about it with excitement, but most of all the pearl buyers knew about it, and when the day had come, in the offices of the pearl buyers, each man sat alone with his little black velvet tray, and each man rolled the pearls about with his finger-tips and considered his part in the picture.

It was supposed that the pearl buyers were individuals

acting alone, bidding against one another for the pearls the fishermen brought in. And once it had been so. But this was a wasteful method, for often, in the excitement of bidding for a pearl, too great a price had been paid to the fishermen. This was extravagant and not to be countenanced. Now there was only one pearl buyer with many hands, and the men who sat in their offices and waited for Kino knew what price they would offer, how high they would bid, and what method each one would use. And although these men would not profit beyond their salaries, there was excitement among the pearl buyers, for there was excitement in the hunt, and if it be a man's function to break down a price, then he must take joy and satisfaction in breaking it as far down as possible. For every man in the world functions to the best of his ability, and no one does less than his best, no matter what he may think about it. Quite apart from any reward they might get, from any word of praise, from any promotion, a pearl buyer was a pearl buyer, and the best and happiest pearl buyer was he who bought for the lowest prices.

The sun was hot yellow that morning, and it drew the moisture from the estuary and from the Gulf and hung it in shimmering scarves in the air so that the air vibrated and vision was unsubstantial. A vision hung in the air to the north of the city – the vision of a mountain that was over two hundred miles away, and the high slopes of this mountain were swaddled with pines and a great stone peak arose above the timber line.

And the morning of this day the canoes lay lined up on

the beach; the fishermen did not go out to dive for pearls, for there would be too much happening, too many things to see when Kino went to sell the great pearl.

In the brush houses by the shore Kino's neighbours sat long over their breakfasts, and they spoke of what they would do if they had found the pearl. And. one man said he would give it as a present to the Holy Father in Rome. Another said that he would buy masses for the souls of his family for a thousand years. Another thought he might take the money and distribute it among the poor of La Paz; and a fourth thought of all the good things one could do with the money from the pearl, of all the charities, benefits, of all the rescues one could perform if one had money. All of the neighbours hoped that sudden wealth would not turn Kino's head, would not make a rich man of him, would not graft on to him the evil limbs of greed and hatred and coldness. For Kino was a well-liked man; it would be a shame if the pearl destroyed him. 'That good wife Juana,' they said, 'and the beautiful baby Coyotito, and the others to come. What a pity it would be if the pearl should destroy them all.'

For Kino and Juana this was the morning of mornings of their lives, comparable only to the day when the baby had been born. This was to be the day from which all other days would take their arrangement. Thus they would say, 'It was two years before we sold the pearl,' or, 'It was six weeks after we sold the pearl.' Juana, considering the matter, threw caution to the winds, and she dressed Coyotito in the clothes she had prepared for

65

his baptism, when there would be money for his baptism. And Juana combed and braided her hair and tied the ends with two little bows of red ribbon, and she put on her marriage skirt and waist. The sun was quarter high when they were ready. Kino's ragged white clothes were clean at least, and this was the last day of his raggedness. For tomorrow, or even this afternoon, he would have new clothes.

The neighbours, watching Kino's door through the crevices in their brush houses, were dressed and ready too. There was no self-consciousness about their joining Kino and Juana to go pearl selling. It was expected, it was an historic moment, they would be crazy if they didn't go. It would be almost a sign of unfriendship.

Juana put on her head-shawl carefully, and she draped one long end under her right elbow and gathered it with her right hand so that a hammock hung under her arm, and in this little hammock she placed Coyotito, propped up against the head-shawl so that he could see everything and perhaps remember. Kino put on his large straw hat and felt it with his hand to see that it was properly placed, not on the back or side of his head, like a rash, unmarried, irresponsible man, and not flat as an elder would wear it, but tilted a little forward to show aggressiveness and seriousness and vigour. There is a great deal to be seen in the tilt of a hat on a man. Kino slipped his feet into his sandals and pulled the thongs up over his heels. The great pearl was wrapped in an old soft piece of deerskin and placed in a little leather bag, and the leather bag was in a pocket in Kino's shirt. He folded his blanket carefully and draped it in a narrow strip over his left shoulder, and now they were ready.

Kino stepped with dignity out of the house, and Juana followed him, carrying Coyotito. And as they marched up the freshet-washed alley towards the town, the neighbours joined them. The houses belched people; the doorways spewed out children. But because of the seriousness of the occasion, only one man walked with Kino, and that was his brother, Juan Tomás.

Juan Tomás cautioned his brother. 'You must be careful to see they do not cheat you,' he said.

And, 'Very careful,' Kino agreed.

'We do not know what prices are paid in other places,' said Juan Tomás. 'How can we know what is a fair price, if we do not know what the pearl buyer gets for the pearl in another place?'

'That is true,' said Kino, 'but how can we know? We are here, we are not there.'

As they walked up towards the city the crowd grew behind them, and Juan Tomás, in pure nervousness, went on speaking.

'Before you were born, Kino,' he said, 'the old ones thought of a way to get more money for their pearls. They thought it would be better if they had an agent who took all the pearls to the capital and sold them there and kept only his share of the profit.'

Kino nodded his head. 'I know,' he said. 'It was a good thought.'

'And so they got such a man,' said Juan Tomás, 'and they pooled the pearls, and they started him off. And he was never heard of again and the pearls were lost. Then they got another man, and they started him off, and he was never heard of again. And so they gave the whole thing up and went back to the old way.'

'I know,' said Kino. 'I have heard our father tell of it. It was a good idea, but it was against religion, and the Father made that very clear. The loss of the pearl was a punishment visited on those who tried to leave their station. And the Father made it clear that each man and woman is like a soldier sent by God to guard some part of the castle of the Universe. And some are in the ramparts and some far deep in the darkness of the walls. But each one must remain faithful to his post and must not go running about, else the castle is in danger from the assaults of Hell.'

'I have heard him make that sermon,' said Juan Tomás. 'He makes it every year.'

The brothers, as they walked along, squinted their eyes a little, as they and their grandfathers and their great-grandfathers had done for four hundred years, since first the strangers came with argument and authority, and gunpowder to back up both. And in the four hundred years Kino's people had learned only one defence – a slight slitting of the eyes and a slight tightening of the lips and a retirement. Nothing could break down this wall, and they could remain whole within the wall.

The gathering procession was solemn, for they sensed

68

the importance of this day, and any children who showed a tendency to scuffle, to scream, to cry out, to steal hats and rumple hair, were hissed to silence by their elders. So important was this day that an old man came~ to see, riding on the stalwart shoulders of his nephew. The procession left the brush huts and entered the stone and plaster city, where the streets were a little wider and there were narrow pavements beside the buildings. And, as before, the beggars joined them as they passed the church; the grocers looked out at them as they went by; the little saloons lost their customers and the owners closed up shop and went along. And the sun beat down on the streets of the city and even tiny stones threw shadows on the ground.

The news of the approach of the procession ran ahead of it, and in their little dark offices the pearl buyers stiffened and grew alert. They got out papers so that they could be at work when Kino appeared, and they put their pearls in the desks, for it is not good to let an inferior pearl be seen beside a beauty. And word of the loveliness of Kino's pearl had come to them. The pearl buyers' offices were clustered together in one narrow street, and they were barred at the windows, and wooden slats cut out the light so that only a soft gloom entered the offices.

A stout slow man sat in an office waiting. His face was fatherly and benign, and his eyes twinkled with friendship. He was a caller of good-mornings, a ceremonious shaker of hands, a jolly man who knew all jokes and yet who hovered close to sadness, for in the midst of a laugh he could remember the death of your aunt, and his eyes could become wet with sorrow for your loss. This morning he had placed a flower in a vase on his desk, a single scarlet hibiscus, and the vase sat beside the black velvet-lined pearl tray in front of him. He was shaved close to the blue roots of his beard, and his hands were clean and his nails polished. His door stood open to the morning, and he hummed under his breath while his right hand practised legerdemain. He rolled a coin back and forth over his knuckles and made it appear and disappear, made it spin and sparkle. The coin winked into sight and as quickly slipped out of sight, and the man did not even watch his own performance. The fingers did it all mechanically, precisely, while the man hummed to himself and peered out the door. Then he heard the tramp of feet of the approaching crowd, and the fingers of his right hand worked faster and faster until, as the figure of Kino filled the doorway, the coin flashed and disappeared.

'Good morning, my friend,' the stout man said. 'What can I do for you?'

Kino stared into the dimness of the little office, for his eyes were squeezed from the outside glare. But the buyer's eyes had become as steady and cruel and unwinking as a hawk's eyes, while the rest of his face smiled in greeting. And secretly, behind his desk, his right hand practised with the coin.

'I have a pearl,' said Kino. And Juan Tomás stood beside him and snorted a little at the understatement. The neighbours peered around the doorway, and a line of little boys clambered on the window bars and looked through. Several little boys, on their hands and knees, watched the scene around Kino's legs.

'You have a pearl,' the dealer said. 'Sometimes a man brings in a dozen. Well, let us see your pearl. We will value it and give you the best price.' And his fingers worked furiously with the coin.

Now, Kino instinctively knew his own dramatic effects. Slowly he brought out the leather bag, slowly took from it the soft and dirty piece of deerskin, and then he let the great pearl roll into the black velvet tray, and instantly his eyes went to the buyer's face. But there was no sign, no movement, the face did not change, but the secret hand behind the desk missed in its precision. The coin stumbled over a knuckle and slipped silently into the dealer's lap. And the fingers behind the desk curled into a fist. When the right hand came out of hiding, the forefinger touched the great pearl, rolled it on the black velvet; thumb and forefinger picked it up and brought it near to the dealer's eyes and twirled it in the air.

Kino held his breath, and the neighbours held their breath, and the whispering went back through the crowd: 'He is inspecting it – No price has been mentioned yet – They have not come to a price.'

Now the dealer's hand had become a personality. The hand tossed the great pearl back in the tray, the forefinger poked and insulted it, and on the dealer's face there came a sad and contemptuous smile.

'I am sorry, my friend,' he said, and his shoulders rose a little to indicate that the misfortune was no fault of his.

'It is a pearl of great value,' Kino said.

The dealer's fingers spurned the pearl so that it bounced and rebounded softly from the side of the velvet tray.

'You have heard of fool's gold,' the dealer said. 'This pearl is like fool's gold. It is too large. Who would buy it? There is no market for such things. It is a curiosity only. I am sorry. You thought it was a thing of value, and it is only a curiosity.'

Now Kino's face was perplexed and worried. 'It is the Pearl of the World,' he cried. 'No one has ever seen such a pearl.'

'On the contrary,' said the dealer, 'it is large and clumsy. As a curiosity it has interest; some museum might perhaps take it in a collection of sea-shells. I can give you, say, a thousand pesos.'

Kino's face grew dark and dangerous. 'It is worth fifty thousand,' he said. 'You know it. You want to cheat me.'

And the dealer heard a little grumble go through the crowd as they heard his price. And the dealer felt a little tremor of fear.

'Do not blame me,' he said quickly. 'I am only an appraiser. Ask the others. Go to their offices and show your pearl – or better, let them come here, so that you can see there is no collusion. Boy,' he called. And when his servant looked through the rear door, 'Boy, go to such a one, and such another and such a third one. Ask them to step in here and do not tell them why. Just say that I will be pleased to see them.' And his right hand went behind the desk and pulled another coin from his pocket, and the coin rolled back and forth over the knuckles.

Kino's neighbours whispered together. They had been afraid of something like this. The pearl was large, but it had a strange colour. They had been suspicious of it from the first. And, after all, a thousand pesos was not to be thrown away. It was comparative wealth to a man who was not wealthy. And suppose Kino took a thousand pesos. Only yesterday he had nothing.

But Kino had grown tight and hard. He felt the creeping of fate, the circling of wolves, the hover of vultures. He felt the evil coagulating about him, and he was helpless to protect himself. He heard in his ears the evil music. And on the black velvet the great pearl glistened, so that the dealer could not keep his eyes from it.

The crowd in the doorway wavered and broke and let the three pearl dealers through. The crowd was silent now, fearing to miss a word, to fail to see a gesture or an expression. Kino was silent and watchful. He felt a little tugging at his back, and he turned and looked in Juana's eyes, and when he looked away he had renewed strength.

The dealers did not glance at one another nor at the pearl. The man behind the desk said, 'I have put a value on this pearl. The owner here does not think it fair. I will ask you to examine this – this thing, and make an offer. Notice,' he said to Kino, 'I have not mentioned what I offered.'

73

The first dealer, dry and stringy, seemed now to see the pearl for the first time. He took it up, rolled it quickly between thumb and forefinger, and then cast it contemptuously back into the tray.

'Do not include me in the discussion,' he said drily. 'I will make no offer at all. I do not want it. This is not a pearl – it is a monstrosity.' His thin lips curled.

Now the second dealer, a little man with a shy soft voice, took up the pearl, and he examined it carefully. He took a glass from his pocket and inspected it under magnification. Then he laughed softly.

'Better pearls are made of paste,' he said. 'I know these things. This is soft and chalky, it will lose its colour and die in a few months. Look –', He offered the glass to Kino, showed him how to use it, and Kino, who had never seen a pearl's surface magnified, was shocked at the strange-looking surface.

The third dealer took the pearl from Kino's hands. 'One of my clients likes such things,' he said. 'I will offer five hundred pesos, and perhaps I can sell it to my client for six hundred.'

Kino reached quickly and snatched the pearl from his hand. He wrapped it in the deerskin and thrust it inside his shirt.

The man behind the desk said, 'I'm a fool, I know, but my first offer stands. I still offer one thousand. What are you doing?' he asked, as Kino thrust the pearl out of sight.

'I am cheated,' Kino cried fiercely. 'My pearl is not for sale here. I will go, perhaps even to the capital.'

Now the dealers glanced quickly at one another. They knew they had played too hard; they knew they would be disciplined for their failure, and the man at the desk said quickly, 'I might go to fifteen hundred.'

But Kino was pushing his way through the crowd. The hum of talk came to him dimly, in his rage blood pounded in his ears, and he burst through and strode away. Juana followed, trotting after him.

When the evening came, the neighbours in the brush houses sat eating their corn-cakes and beans, and they discussed the great theme of the morning. They did not know, it seemed a fine pearl to them, but they had never seen such a pearl before, and surely the dealers knew more about the value of pearls than they. 'And mark this,' they said. 'Those dealers did not discuss these things. Each of the three knew the pearl was valueless.'

'But suppose they had arranged it before?'

'If that is so, then all of us have been cheated all of our lives.'

Perhaps, some argued, perhaps it would have been better if Kino took the one thousand five hundred pesos. That is a great deal of money, more than he has ever seen. Maybe Kino is being a pig-headed fool. Suppose he should really go to the capital and find no buyer for his pearl. He would never live that down.

And now, said other fearful ones, now that he had defied them, those buyers will not want to deal with him at all. Maybe Kino has cut off his own head and destroyed himself.

And others said, Kino is a brave man, and a fierce man; he is right. From his courage we may all profit. These were proud of Kino.

In his house Kino squatted on his sleeping-mat, brooding. He had buried his pearl under a stone of the fire hole in his house, and he stared at the woven tules of his sleeping-mat until the crossed design danced in his head. He had lost one world and had not gained another. And Kino was afraid. Never in his life had he been far from home. He was afraid of strangers and of strange places. He was terrified of that monster of strangeness they called the capital. It lay over the water and through the mountains, over a thousand miles, and every strange terrible mile was frightening. But Kino had lost his old world and he must clamber on to a new one. For his dream of the future was real and never to be destroyed, and he had said 'I will go', and that made a real thing too. To determine to go and to say it was to be halfway there.

Juana watched him while he buried his pearl, and she watched him while she cleaned Coyotito and nursed him, and Juana made the corn-cakes for supper.

Juan Tomás came in and squatted down beside Kino and remained silent for a long time, until at last Kino demanded, "What else could I do? They are cheats.'

Juan Tomás nodded gravely. He was the elder, and Kino looked to him for wisdom. 'It is hard to know,' he said. 'We do know that we are cheated from birth to the overcharge on our coffins. But we survive. You have

76

defied not the pearl buyers, but the whole structure, the whole way of life, and I am afraid for you.'

'What have I to fear but starvation?' Kino asked.

But Juan Tomás shook his head slowly. 'That we must all fear. But suppose you are correct – suppose your pearl is of great value – do you think then the game is over?'

'What do you mean?'

'I don't know,' said Juan Tomás, 'but I am afraid for you. It is new ground you are walking on, you do not know the way.'

'I will go. I will go soon,' said Kino.

'Yes,' Juan Tomás agreed. 'That you must do. But I wonder if you will find it any different in the capital. Here you have friends and me, your brother. There you will have no one.'

'What can I do?' Kino cried. 'Some deep outrage is here. My son must have a chance. That is what they are striking at. My friends will protect me.'

'Only so long as they are not in danger or discomfort from it,' said Juan Tomás. He rose, saying, 'Go with God.'

And Kino said, 'Go with God,' and did not even look up, for the words had a strange chill in them.

Long after Juan Tomás. had gone Kino sat brooding on his sleeping-mat. A lethargy had settled on him, and a little grey hopelessness. Every road seemed blocked against him. In his head he heard only the dark music of the enemy. His senses were burningly alive, but his mind went back to the deep participation with all things, the gift he had from his people. He heard every little sound of the gathering night, the sleepy complaint of settling birds, the love agony of cats, the strike and withdrawal of little waves on the beach, and the simple hiss of distance. And he could smell the sharp odour of exposed kelp from the receding tide. The little flare of the twig fire made the design on his sleeping-mat jump before his entranced eyes.

Juana watched him with worry, but she knew him and she knew she could help him best by being silent and by being near. And as though she too could hear the Song of Evil, she fought it, singing softly the melody of the family, of the safety and warmth and wholeness of the family. She held Coyotito in her arms and sang the song to him, to keep the evil out, and her voice was brave against the threat of the dark music.

Kino did not move nor ask for his supper. She knew he would ask when he wanted it. His eyes were entranced, and he could sense the wary, watchful evil outside the brush house; he could feel the dark creeping things waiting for him to go out into the night. It was shadowy and dreadful, and yet it called to him and threatened him and challenged him. His right hand went into his shirt and felt his knife; his eyes were wide; he stood up and walked to the doorway.

Juana willed to stop him; she raised her hand to stop him, and her mouth opened with terror. For a long moment Kino looked out into the darkness and then he stepped outside. Juana heard the little rush, the grunting struggle, the blow. She froze with terror for a moment, and then her lips drew back from her teeth like a cat's lips. She set Coyotito down on the ground. She seized a stone from the fireplace and rushed outside, but it was over by then. Kino lay on the ground, struggling to rise, and there was no one near him. Only the shadows and the strike and the rush of waves and the hiss of distance.

But the evil was all about, hidden behind the brush fence, crouched beside the house in the shadow, hovering in the air.

Juana dropped her stone, and she put her arms around Kino and helped him to his feet and supported him into the house. Blood oozed down from his scalp and there was a long deep cut in his cheek from ear to chin, a deep, bleeding slash. And Kino was only half conscious. He shook his head from side to side. His shirt was torn open and his clothes half pulled *off*. Juana sat him down on his sleeping-mat and she wiped the thickening blood from his face with her skirt. She brought him pulque to drink in a little pitcher, and still he shook his head to clear out the darkness.

'Who?' Juana asked.

'I don't know,' Kino said. 'I didn't see.'

Now Juana brought her clay pot of water and she washed the cut on his face while he stared dazed ahead of him.

'Kino, my husband,' she cried, and his eyes stared past her. 'Kino, can you hear me?'

'I hear you,' he said dully.

'Kino, this pearl is evil. Let us destroy it before it

destroys us. Let us crush it between two stones. Let us –
let us throw it back in the sea where it belongs. Kino, it is
evil, it is evil!'

And as she spoke the light came back in Kino's eyes so
that they glowed fiercely and his muscles hardened and
his will hardened.

'No,' he said. 'I will fight this thing. I will win over it.
We will have our chance.' His fist pounded the sleeping-
mat. 'No one shall take our good fortune from us,' he said.
His eyes softened then and he raised a gentle hand to
Juana's shoulder. 'Believe me,' he said. 'I am a man.' And
his face grew crafty.

'In the morning we will take our canoe and we will go
over the sea and over the mountains to the capital, you
and I. We will not be cheated. I am a man.'

'Kino,' she said huskily, 'I am afraid. A man can be
killed. Let us throw the pearl back into the sea.'

'Hush,' he said fiercely. 'I am a man. Hush.' And she
was silent, for his voice was command. 'Let us sleep a
little,' he said. 'In the first light we will start. You are not
afraid to go with me?'

'No, my husband.'

His eyes were soft and warm on her then, his hand
touched her cheek. 'Let us sleep a little,' he said.

Notes for Chapter 5

While Kino and Coyotito are asleep, Juana takes the pearl and tries to throw it into the sea. Kino catches her and attackes her. Later he is attacked and stabs his assailant. Juana finds Kino lying semi-conscious in the pathway. They decide to escape in the canoe, but Kino finds that someone has knocked a hole in it. The hut is set on fire, but they escape and hide in Juan Tomás' house.

What do you think?

Think how the pearl has changed both Kino and Juana, making them even less open with each other and, in Kino's case, more inclined to violence. Think also how, during the progress of the story, Juana has become more forceful and less submissive to Kino's wishes.

Questions

1. What makes Juana continue to protect Kino and the pearl, even after he has beaten her?
2. What do you think Steinbeck means when he writes, 'Now, in an instant, Juana knew that the old life was gone for ever.'? What was the old life and how has it changed?
3. When Kino says 'I am a man', what does he mean by this? How does Juana interpret his meaning differently?
4. What does Kino mean when he says to Juan Tomás, 'I know I am like a leprosy.'?
5. Despite all the grief it has brought him, Kino decides to keep the pearl. Why?

Further activity

Imagine that you are a reporter for the local newspaper. Write an article telling the story of Kino's discovery. Include interviews with local people, but remember that you would be unlikely, as a Spanish Mexican, to visit the native village. Set out your article in a suitable format with an eye-catching headline. If you can, use a DTP program to help you with the layout and presentation of your work. You may wish to work with a partner to produce a complete front page of your newspaper.

Chapter 5

The late moon arose before the first rooster crowed. Kino opened his eyes in the darkness, for he sensed movement near him, but he did not move. Only his eyes searched the darkness, and in the pale light of the moon that crept through the holes in the brush house Kino saw Juana arise silently from beside him. He saw her move towards the fireplace. So carefully did she work that he heard only the lightest sound when she moved the fireplace stone. And then like a shadow she glided towards the door. She paused for a moment beside the hanging box where Coyotito lay, then for a second she was black in the doorway, and then she was gone.

And rage surged in Kino. He rolled up to his feet and followed her as silently as she had gone, and he could hear her quick footsteps going towards the shore. Quietly he tracked her, and his brain was red with anger. She burst clear out of the brush line and stumbled over the little boulders towards the water, and then she heard him coming and she broke into a run. Her arm was up to throw when he leaped at her and caught her arm and wrenched the pearl from her. He struck her in the face with his clenched fist and she fell among the boulders, and he kicked her in the side. In the pale light he could see the little waves break over her, and her skirt floated about and clung to her legs as the water receded.

Kino looked down at her and his teeth were bared. He hissed at her like a snake, and Juana stared at him with wide unfrightened eyes, like a sheep before the butcher. She knew there was murder in him, and it was all right; she had accepted it, and she would not resist or even protest. And then the rage left him and a sick disgust took its place. He turned away from her and walked up the beach and through the brush line. His senses were dulled by his emotion.

He heard the rush, got his knife out and lunged at one dark figure and felt his knife go home, and then he was swept to his knees and swept again to the ground. Greedy fingers went through his clothes, frantic fingers searched him, and the pearl, knocked from his hand, lay winking behind a little stone in the pathway. It glinted in the soft moonlight.

Juana dragged herself up from the rocks on the edge of the water. Her face was a dull pain and her side ached. She steadied herself on her knees for a while and her wet skirt clung to her. There was no anger in her for Kino. He had said, 'I am a man,' and that meant certain things to Juana. It meant that he was half insane and half god. It meant that Kino would drive his strength against a mountain and plunge his strength against the sea. Juana, in her woman's soul, knew that the mountain would stand while the man broke himself; that the sea would surge while the man drowned in it. And yet it was this thing that made him a man, half insane and half god, and Juana had need of a man; she could not live without a man. Although she might be puzzled by these differences between man and woman, she knew them and accepted them and needed them. Of course she would follow him, there was no question of that. Sometimes the quality of woman, the reason, the caution, the sense of preservation, could cut through Kino's manness and save them all. She climbed painfully to her feet, and she dipped her cupped palms in the little waves and washed her bruised face with the stinging salt water, and then she went creeping up the beach after Kino.

A flight of herring clouds had moved over the sky from the south. The pale moon dipped in and out of the strands of clouds so that Juana walked in darkness for a moment and in light the next. Her back was bent with pain and her head was low. She went through the line of brush when the moon was covered, and when it looked through she saw the glimmer of the great pearl in the path behind the rock. She sank to her knees and picked it up, and the moon went into the darkness of the clouds again. Juana remained on her knees while she considered whether to go back to the sea and finish her job, and as she considered, the light came again, and she saw two dark figures lying in the path ahead of her. She leaped forward and saw that one was Kino and the other a stranger with dark shiny fluid leaking from his throat.

Kino moved sluggishly, arms and legs stirred like those of a crushed bug, and a thick muttering came from his mouth. Now, in an instant, Juana knew that the old life was gone for ever. A dead man in the path and Kino's knife, dark-bladed beside him, convinced her. All of the time Juana had been trying to rescue something of the old peace, of the time before the pearl. But now it was gone, and there was no retrieving it. And, knowing this, she abandoned the past instantly. There was nothing to do but to save themselves.

Her pain was gone now, her slowness. Quickly she dragged the dead man from the pathway into the shelter of the brush. She went to Kino and sponged his face with her wet skirt. His senses were coming back and he moaned.

'They have taken the pearl. I have lost it. Now it is over,' he said. 'The pearl is gone.'

Juana quieted him as she would quiet a sick child. 'Hush,' she said. 'Here is your pearl. I found it in the path. Can you hear me now? Here is your pearl. Can you understand? You have killed a man. We must go away. They will come for us, can you understand? We must be gone before the daylight comes.'

'I was attacked,' Kino said uneasily. 'I struck to save my life.'

'Do you remember yesterday?' Juana asked. 'Do you think that will matter? Do you remember the men of the city? Do you think your explanation will help?'

Kino drew a great breath and fought off his weakness. 'No,' he said. 'You are right.' And his will hardened and he was a man again.

'Go to our house and bring Coyotito,' he said, 'and bring all the corn we have. I will drag the canoe into the water and we will go.'

He took his knife and left her. He stumbled towards the

beach and he came to his canoe. And when the light broke through again he saw that a great hole had been knocked in the bottom. And a searing rage came to him and gave him strength. Now the darkness was closing in on his family; now the evil music filled the night, hung over the mangroves, swirled in the wave-beat. The canoe of his grandfather, plastered over and over, and a splintered hole broken in it. This was an evil beyond thinking. The killing of a man was not so evil as the killing of a boat. For a boat does not have sons, and a boat cannot protect itself, and a wounded boat does not heal. There was sorrow in Kino's rage, but this last thing had tightened him beyond breaking. He was an animal now, for hiding, for attacking, and he lived only to preserve himself and his family. He was not conscious of the pain in his head. He leaped up the beach, through the brush line towards his brush house, and it did not occur to him to take one of the canoes of his neighbours. Never once did the thought enter his head, any more than he could have conceived breaking a boat.

The roosters were crowing and the dawn was not far off. Smoke of the first fires seeped out through the walls of the brush houses, and the first smell of cooking corn-cakes was in the air. Already the dawn birds were scampering in the bushes. The weak moon was losing its light and the clouds thickened and curdled to the southward. The wind blew freshly into the estuary, a nervous, restless wind with the smell of storm on its breath, and there was change and uneasiness in the air.

Kino, hurrying towards his house, felt a surge of exhilaration. Now he was not confused, for there was only one thing to do, and Kino's hand went first to the great pearl in his shirt and then to his knife hanging under his shirt.

He saw a little glow ahead of him, and then without interval a tall flame leaped up in the dark with a crackling roar, and a tall edifice of fire lighted the pathway. Kino broke into a run; it was his brush house, he knew. And he knew that these houses could burn down in a very few moments. And as he ran a scuttling figure ran towards him – Juana, with Coyotito in her arms and Kino's shoulder-blanket clutched in her hand. The baby moaned with fright, and Juana's eyes were wide and terrified. Kino could see the house was gone, and he did not question Juana. He knew, but she said, 'It was torn up and the floor dug – even the baby's box turned out, and as I looked they put the fire to the outside.'

The fierce light of the burning house lighted Kino's face strongly. 'Who?' he demanded.

'I don't know,' she said. 'The dark ones.'

The neighbours were tumbling from their houses now, and they watched the falling sparks and stamped them out to save their own houses. Suddenly Kino was afraid. The light made him afraid. He remembered the man lying dead in the brush beside the path, and he took Juana by the arm and drew her into the shadow of a house away from the light, for light was danger to him. For a moment he considered and then he worked among the shadows until he came to the house of Juan Tomás, his brother, and he slipped into the doorway and drew Juana with him. Outside, he could hear the squeal of children and the shouts of the neighbours, for his friends thought he might be inside the burning house.

The house of Juan Tomás was almost exactly like Kino's house; nearly all the brush houses were alike, and all leaked light and air, so that Juana and Kino, sitting in the corner of the brother's house, could see the leaping flames through the wall. They saw the flames tall and furious, they saw the roof fall and watched the fire die down as quickly as a twig fire dies. They heard the cries of warning of their friends, and the shrill, keening cry of Apolonia, wife of Juan Tomás. She, being the nearest woman relative, raised a formal lament for the dead of the family.

Apolonia realised that she was wearing her second-best head-shawl and she rushed to her house to get her fine new one. As she rummaged in a box by the wall, Kino's voice said quietly, 'Apolonia, do not cry out. We are not hurt.'

'How do you come here?' she demanded.

'Do not question,' he said. 'Go now to Juan Tomás and bring him here and tell no one else. This is important to us, Apolonia.'

She paused, her hands helpless in front of her, and then, 'Yes, my brother-in-law,' she said.

In a few moments Juan Tomás came back with her. He lighted a candle and came to them where they crouched in a corner, and he said, 'Apolonia, see to the door, and do not let anyone enter.' He was older, Juan Tomás, and he assumed the authority. 'Now, my brother,' he said.

'I was attacked in the dark,' said Kino. 'And in the fight I have killed a man.'

'Who?' asked Juan Tomás quickly.

'I do not know. It is all darkness – all darkness and shape of darkness.'

'It is the pearl,' said Juan Tomás. 'There is a devil in this pearl. You should have sold it and passed on the devil. Perhaps you can still sell it and buy peace for yourself.'

And Kino said, 'Oh, my brother, an insult has been put on me that is deeper than my life. For on the beach my canoe is broken, my house is burned, and in the brush a dead man lies. Every escape is cut off. You must hide us, my brother.'

And Kino, looking closely, saw deep worry come into his brother's eyes and he forestalled him in a possible refusal. 'Not for long,' he said quickly. 'Only until a day has passed and the new light has come. Then we will go.'

'I will hide you,' said Juan Tomas.

'I do not want to bring danger to you,' Kino said. 'I know I am like a leprosy. I will go tonight and then you will be safe.'

'I will protect you,' said Juan Tomás, and he called, 'Apolonia, close up the door. Do not even whisper that Kino is here.'

They sat silently all day in the darkness of the house, and they could hear the neighbours speaking of them. Through the walls of the house they could watch their neighbours raking through the ashes to find the bones.

Crouching in the house of Juan Tomás, they heard the shock go into their neighbours' minds at the news of the broken boat. Juan Tomás went out among the neighbours to divert their suspicions, and he gave them theories and ideas of what had happened to Kino and Juana and to the baby. To one he said, 'I think they have gone south along the coast to escape the evil that was on them.' And to another, 'Kino would never leave the sea. Perhaps he has found another boat.' And he said, 'Apolonia is ill with grief.'

And in that day the wind rose up to beat the Gulf and tore the kelps and weeds that lined the shore, and the wind cried through the brush houses and no boat was safe on the water. Then Juan Tomás told among the neighbours: 'Kino is gone. If he went to the sea, he is drowned by now.' And after each trip among the neighbours Juan Tomás came back with something borrowed. He brought a little woven straw bag of red beans and a gourd full of rice. He borrowed a cup of dried peppers and a block of salt, and he brought in a long working knife, eighteen inches long and heavy, as a small axe, a tool and a weapon. And when Kino saw this knife his eyes lighted up, and he fondled the blade and his thumb tested the edge.

The wind screamed over the Gulf and turned the water white, and the mangroves plunged like frightened cattle, and a fine sandy dust arose from the land and hung in a

91

stifling cloud over the sea. The wind drove off the clouds and skimmed the sky clean and drifted the sand of the country like snow.

Then Juan Tomás, when the evening approached, talked long with his brother. 'Where will you go?'

'To the north,' said Kino. 'I have heard that there are cities in the north.'

'Avoid the shore,' said Juan Tomás. 'They are making a party to search the shore. The men in the city will look for you. Do you still have the pearl?'

'I have it,' said Kino. 'And I will keep it. I might have given it as a gift, but now it is my misfortune and my life and I will keep it.' His eyes were hard and cruel and bitter.

Coyotito whimpered and Juana muttered little magics over him to make him silent.

'The wind is good,' said Juan Tomás. 'There will be no tracks.'

They left quietly in the dark before the moon had risen. The family stood formally in the house of Juan Tomás. Juana carried Coyotito on her back, covered and held in by her head-shawl, and the baby slept, cheek turned sideways against her shoulder. The head-shawl covered the baby, and one end of it came across Juana's nose to protect her from the evil night air. Juan Tomás embraced his brother with the double embrace and kissed him on both cheeks. 'Go with God,' he said, and it was like a death. 'You will not give up the pearl?'

'This pearl has become my soul,' said Kino. 'If I give it up I shall lose my soul. Go thou also with God.'

Notes for Chapter 6

Kino and Juana set out to escape to the north. Kino tries to cover their tracks. As day breaks they hide in a thicket near the road. Kino awakes and sees three trackers pursuing them. He leads Juana further into the mountains until they come to a ravine where they hide. Kino attacks his pursuers and kills all three, but in the struggle Coyotito is killed by a stray bullet. Kino and Juana return to the village and throw the pearl back into the sea.

What do you think?
Why does Kino not go to the police for protection for himself and his family?

Questions
1. Earlier Kino and Juana believed the night air to be evil. What changes can you see in them as they begin their night-time escape?
2. As they hide from their pursuers, how does Kino try to convince himself and Juana that they are right to run away?
3. Why does Juana refuse to leave Kino when he tells her to hide? Has anything occurred earlier to explain her stubbornness now?
4. How do you think Coyotito's death might have been avoided?
5. Walking through La Paz to throw the pearl into the sea, Kino 'was immune and terrible, and his song had become a battle cry'. What battle was Kino fighting?

Further activity
Steinbeck ends the story by returning the pearl to the sea. What might Kino and Juana have done after this? Write a further short chapter to show how they had learned from their experiences. Amongst other points you might wish to include some references to: Coyotito's burial; the rebuilding of their hut; the sort of welcome they may have received from Juan Tomás and Apolonia; what Kino did with the rifle; how he repaired his canoe; changes Kino and Juana might have made in their way of life. Try to make your chapter fit in with the book's style, as regard description and dialogue.

Chapter 6

The wind blew fierce and strong, and it pelted them with bits of sticks, sand, and little rocks. Juana and Kino gathered their clothing tighter about them and covered their noses and went out into the world. The sky was brushed clean by the wind and the stars were cold in a black sky. The two walked carefully, and they avoided the centre of the town, where some sleeper in a doorway might see them pass. For the town closed itself in against the night, and anyone who moved about in the darkness would be noticeable. Kino threaded his way around the edge of the city and turned north, north by the stars, and found the rutted sandy road that led through the brushy country towards Loreto, where the miraculous Virgin has her station.

Kino could feel the blown sand against his ankles and he was glad, for he knew there would be no tracks. The little light from the stars made out for him the narrow road through the brushy country. And Kino could hear the pad of Juana's feet behind him. He went quickly and quietly, and Juana trotted behind him to keep up.

Some ancient thing stirred in Kino. Through his fear of dark and the devils that haunt the night, there came a rush of exhilaration; some animal thing was moving in him so that he was cautious and wary and dangerous; some ancient thing out of the past of his people was alive in him. The wind was at his back and the stars guided him. The wind cried and whisked in the brush, and the family went on monotonously, hour after hour. They passed no one and saw no one. At last, to their right, the waning moon arose, and when it came up the wind died down, and the land was still.

Now they could see the little road ahead of them, deep cut with sand-drifted wheel tracks. With the wind gone there would be footprints, but they were a good distance from the town and perhaps their tracks might not be noticed. Kino walked carefully in a wheel-rut, and Juana followed in his path. One big cart, going to the town in the morning, could wipe out every trace of their passage.

All night they walked and never changed their pace. Once Coyotito awakened, and Juana shifted him in front of her and soothed him until he went to sleep again. And the evils of the night were about them. The coyotes cried and laughed in the brush, and the owls screeched and hissed over their heads. And once some large animal lumbered away, crackling the undergrowth as it went. And Kino gripped the handle of the big working knife and took a sense of protection from it.

The music of the pearl was triumphant in Kino's head, and the quiet melody of the family underlay it, and they wove themselves into the soft padding of sandalled feet in the dust. All night they walked, and in the first dawn Kino searched the roadside for a covert to lie in during the day. He found his place near to the road, a little clearing where deer might have lain, and it was curtained thickly with the dry brittle trees that lined the road. And when Juana had seated herself and had settled to nurse the baby, Kino went back to the road. He broke a branch and carefully swept the footprints where they had turned from the roadway. And then, in the first light, he heard the creak of a wagon, and he crouched beside the road and watched a heavy two-wheeled cart go by, drawn by slouching oxen. And when it had passed out of sight, he went back to the roadway and looked at the rut and found that the footprints were gone. And again he swept out his traces and went back to Juana.

She gave him the soft corn-cakes Apolonia had packed for them, and after a while she slept a little. But Kino sat on the ground and stared at the earth in front of him. He watched the ants moving, a little column of them near to his foot, and he put his foot in their path. Then the column climbed over his instep and continued on its way, and Kino left his foot there and watched them move over it.

The sun arose hotly. They were not near the Gulf now, and the air was dry and hot so that the brush cricked with heat and a good resinous smell came from it. And when Juana awakened, when the sun was high, Kino told her things she knew already.

'Beware of that kind of tree there,' he said, pointing. 'Do not touch it, for if you do and then touch your eyes, it will blind you. And beware of the tree that bleeds. See, that one over there. For if you break it the red blood will flow from it, and it is evil luck.' And she nodded and smiled a little at him, for she knew these things.

'Will they follow us?' she asked. 'Do you think they will try to find us?'

97

'They will try,' said Kino. 'Whoever finds us will take the pearl. Oh, they will try.'

And Juana said, 'Perhaps the dealers were right and the pearl has no value. Perhaps this has all been an illusion.'

Kino reached into his clothes and brought out the pearl. He let the sun play on it until it burned in his eyes. 'No,' he said, 'they would not have tried to steal it if it had been valueless.'

'Do you know who attacked you? Was it the dealers?'

'I do not know,' he said. 'I didn't see them.'

He looked into his pearl to find his vision. 'When we sell it at last, I will have a rifle,' he said, and he looked into the shining surface for his rifle, but he saw only a huddled dark body on the ground with shining blood dripping from its throat. And he said quickly, 'We will be married in a great church.' And in the pearl he saw Juana with her beaten face crawling home through the night. 'Our son must learn to read,' he said frantically. And there in the pearl Coyotito's face, thick and feverish from the medicine.

And Kino thrust the pearl back into his clothing, and the music of the pearl had become sinister in his ears, and it was interwoven with the music of evil.

The hot sun beat on the earth so that Kino and Juana moved into the lacy shade of the brush, and small grey birds scampered on the ground in the shade. In the heat of the day Kino relaxed and covered his eyes with his hat and wrapped his blanket about his face to keep the flies off, and he slept.

But Juana did not sleep. She sat quiet as a stone and her face was quiet. Her mouth was still swollen where Kino had struck her, and big flies buzzed around the cut on her chin. But she sat as still as a sentinel, and when Coyotito awakened she placed him on the ground in front of her and watched him wave his arms and kick his feet, and he smiled and gurgled at her until she smiled too. She picked up a little twig from the ground and tickled him, and she gave him water from the gourd she carried in her bundle.

Kino stirred in a dream, and he cried out in a guttural voice, and his hand moved in symbolic fighting. And then he moaned and sat up suddenly, his eyes wide and his nostrils flaring. He listened and heard only the cricking heat and the hiss of distance.

'What is it?' Juana asked.

'Hush,' he said.

'You were dreaming.'

'Perhaps.' But he was restless, and when she gave him a corn-cake from her store he paused in his chewing to listen. He was uneasy and nervous; he glanced over his shoulder; he lifted the big knife and felt its edge. When Coyotito gurgled on the ground Kino said, 'Keep him quiet.'

'What is the matter?' Juana asked.

'I don't know.'

He listened again, an animal light in his eyes. He stood up then, silently; and, crouched low, he threaded his way through the brush towards the road. But he did not step into the road; he crept into the cover of a thorny tree and peered out along the way he had come.

And then he saw them moving along. His body stiffened and he drew down his head and peeked out from under a fallen branch. In the distance he could see three figures, two on foot and one on horseback. But he knew what they were, and a chill of fear went through him. Even in the distance he could see the two on foot moving slowly along, bent low to the ground. Here one would pause and look at the earth, while the other joined him. They were the trackers, they could follow the trail of a bighorn sheep in the stone mountains. They were as sensitive as hounds. Here he and Juana might have stepped out of the wheel rut, and these people from the inland, these hunters, could follow, could read a broken straw or a little tumbled pile of dust. Behind them, on a horse, was a dark man, his nose covered with a blanket, and across his saddle a rifle gleamed in the sun.

Kino lay as rigid as the tree limb. He barely breathed, and his eyes went to the place where he had swept out the track. Even the sweeping might be a message to the trackers. He knew these inland hunters. In a country where there was little game they managed to live because of their ability to hunt, and they were hunting him. They scuttled over the ground like animals and found a sign and crouched over it while the horseman waited.

The trackers whined a little, like excited dogs on a warming trail. Kino slowly drew his big knife to his hand

and made it ready. He knew what he must do. If the trackers found the swept place, he must leap for the horseman, kill him quickly and take the rifle. That was his only chance in the world. And as the three drew nearer on the road, Kino dug little pits with his sandalled toes so that he could leap without warning, so that his feet would not slip. He had only a little vision under the fallen limb.

Now Juana, back in her hidden place, heard the pad of the horse's hoofs, and Coyotito gurgled. She took him up quickly and put him under her shawl and gave him her breast and he was silent.

When the trackers came near, Kino could see only their legs and only the legs of the horse from under the fallen branch. He saw the dark horny feet of the men and their ragged white clothes, and he heard the creak of leather of the saddle and the clink of spurs. The trackers stopped at the swept place and studied it, and the horseman stopped. The horse flung his head up against the bit and the bit-roller clicked under his tongue and the horse snorted. Then the dark trackers turned and studied the horse and watched his ears.

Kino was not breathing, but his back arched a little and the muscles of his arms and legs stood out with tension and a line of sweat formed on his upper lip. For a long moment the trackers bent over the road, and then they moved on slowly, studying the ground ahead of them, and the horseman moved after them. The trackers scuffled along, stopping, looking, and hurrying on. They would be back, Kino knew. They would be circling and searching, peeping, stooping, and they would come back sooner or later to his covered track.

He slid backwards and did not bother to cover his tracks. He could not; too many little signs were there, too many broken twigs and scuffed places and displaced stones. And there was a panic in Kino now, a panic of flight. The trackers would find his trail, he knew it. There was no escape, except in flight. He edged away from the road and went quickly and silently to the hidden place where Juana was. She looked up at him in question.

'Trackers,' he said. 'Come!'

And then a helplessness and a hopelessness swept over him, and his face went black and his eyes were sad. 'Perhaps I should let them take me.'

Instantly Juana was on her feet and her hand lay on his arm. 'You have the pearl,' she cried hoarsely. 'Do you think they would take you back alive to say they had stolen it?'

His hand strayed limply to the place where the pearl was hidden under his clothes. 'They will find it,' he said weakly.

'Come,' she said. 'Come!'

And when he did not respond: 'Do you think they would let me live? Do you think they would let the little one here live?'

Her goading struck into his brain; his lips snarled and his eyes were fierce again. 'Come,' he said. 'We will go into the mountains. Maybe we can lose them in the mountains.'

Frantically he gathered the gourds and the little bags that were their property. Kino carried a bundle in his left hand, but the big knife swung free in his right hand. He parted the brush for Juana and they hurried to the west, towards the high stone mountains. They trotted quickly through the tangle of the undergrowth. This was panic flight. Kino did not try to conceal his passage; he trotted, kicking the stones, knocking the tell-tale leaves from the little trees. The high sun streamed down on the dry creaking earth so that even the vegetation ticked in protest. But ahead were the naked granite mountains, rising out of erosion rubble and standing monolithic against the sky. And Kino ran for the high place, as nearly all animals do when they are pursued.

This land was waterless, furred with the cacti which could store water and with the great-rooted brush which could reach deep into the earth for a little moisture and get along on very little. And under-foot was not soil but broken rock, split into small cubes, great slabs, but none of it water-rounded. Little tufts of sad dry grass grew between the stones, grass that had sprouted with one single rain and headed, dropped its seed, and died. Horned toads watched the family go by and turned their little pivoting dragon heads. And now and then a great jack-rabbit, disturbed in his sleep, bumped away and hid behind the nearest rock. The singing heat lay over this desert country, and ahead the stone mountains looked cool and welcoming.

And Kino fled. He knew what would happen. A little

103

way along the road the trackers would become aware that they had missed the path, and they would come back, searching and judging, and in a little while they would find the place where Kino and Juana had rested. From there it would be easy for them – these little stones, the fallen leaves and the whipped branches, the scuffed places where a foot had slipped. Kino could see them in his mind, slipping along the track, whining a little with eagerness, and behind them, dark and half-interested, the horseman with the rifle. His work would come last, for he would not take them back. Oh, the music of evil sang loud in Kino's head now, it sang with the whine of heat and with the dry ringing of snake rattles. It was not large and overwhelming now, but secret and poisonous, and the pounding of his heart gave it undertone and rhythm.

The way began to rise, and as it did the rocks grew larger. But now Kino had put a little distance between his family and the trackers. Now, on the first rise, he rested. He climbed a great boulder and looked back over the shimmering country, but he could not see his enemies, not even the tall horseman riding through the brush. Juana had squatted in the shade of the boulder. She raised her bottle of water to Coyotito's lips; his little dried tongue sucked greedily at it. She looked up at Kino when he came back; she saw him examine her ankles, cut and scratched from the stones and brush, and she covered them quickly with her skirt. Then she handed the bottle to him, but he shook his head. Her eyes were bright in her tired face. Kino moistened his cracked lips with his tongue.

'Juana,' he said, 'I will go on and you will hide. I will lead them into the mountains, and when they have gone past, you will go north to Loreto or to Santa Rosalia. Then, if I can escape them, I will come to you. It is the only safe way.'

She looked full into his eyes for a moment. 'No,' she said. 'We go with you.'

'I can go faster alone,' he said harshly. 'You will put the little one in more danger if you go with me.'

'No,' said Juana.

'You must. It is the wise thing and it is my wish,' he said.

'No,' said Juana.

He looked then for weakness in her face, for fear or irresolution, and there was none. Her eyes were very bright. He shrugged his shoulders helplessly then, but he had taken strength from her. When they moved on it was no longer panic flight.

The country, as it rose toward the mountains, changed rapidly. Now there were long outcroppings of granite with deep crevices between, and Kino walked on bare unmarkable stone when he could and leaped from ledge to ledge. He knew that wherever the trackers lost his path they must circle and lose time before they found it again. And so he did not go straight for the mountains any more; he moved in zigzags, and sometimes he cut back to the south and left a sign and then went towards the mountains over bare stone again. And the path rose steeply now, so that he panted a little as he went.

The sun moved downwards toward the bare stone teeth of the mountains, and Kino set his direction for a dark and shadowy cleft in the range. If there were any water at all, it would be there, where he could see, even in the distance, a hint of foliage. And if there were any passage through the smooth stone range, it would be by this same deep cleft. It had its danger, for the trackers would think of it too, but the empty water-bottle did not let that consideration enter. And as the sun lowered, Kino and Juana struggled wearily up the steep slope towards the cleft.

High in the grey stone mountains, under a frowning peak, a little spring bubbled out of a rupture in the stone. It was fed by shade-preserved snow in the summer, and now and then it died completely and bare rocks and dry algæ were on its bottom. But nearly always it gushed out, cold and clean and lovely. In the times when the quick rains fell, it might become a freshlet and send its column of white water crashing down the mountain cleft, but nearly always it was a lean little spring. It bubbled out into a pool and then fell a hundred feet to another pool, and this one, overflowing, dropped again, so that it continued, down and down, until it came to the rubble of the upland, and there it disappeared altogether. There wasn't much left of it then anyway, for every time it fell over an escarpment the thirsty air drank it, and it splashed from the pools to the dry vegetation. The animals for miles around came to drink from the little pools, and the wild sheep and the deer, the pumas and raccoons, and the mice

– all came to drink. And the birds which spent the day in the brushland came at night to the little pools that were like steps in the mountain cleft. Beside this tiny stream, wherever enough earth collected for root-hold, colonies of plants grew, wild grape and little palms, maidenhair fern, hibiscus, and tall pampas grass with feathery rods raised above the spike leaves. And in the pool lived frogs and water-skaters, and water-worms crawled on the bottom of the pool. Everything that loved water came to these few shallow places. The cats took their prey there, and strewed feathers and lapped water through their bloody teeth. The little pools were places of life because of the water, and places of killing because of the water, too.

The lowest step, where the stream collected before it tumbled down a hundred feet and disappeared into the rubbly desert, was a little platform of stone and sand.

Only a pencil of water fell into the pool, but it was enough to keep the pool full and to keep the ferns green in the underhang of the cliff, and wild grape climbed the stone mountain and all manner of little plants found comfort here. The freshets had made a small sandy beach through which the pool flowed, and bright-green watercress grew in the damp sand. The beach was cut and scarred and padded by the feet of animals that had come to drink and to hunt.

The sun had passed over the stone mountains when Kino and Juana struggled up the steep broken slope and came at last to the water. From this step they could look out over the sunbeaten desert to the blue Gulf in the distance. They came utterly weary to the pool, and Juana slumped to her knees and first washed Coyotito's face and then filled her bottle and gave him a drink. And the baby was weary and petulant, and he cried softly until Juana gave him her breast, and then he gurgled and clucked against her. Kino drank long and thirstily at the pool. For a moment then he stretched out beside the water and relaxed all his muscles and watched Juana feed the baby, and then he got to his feet and went to the edge of the step where the water slipped over, and he searched the distance carefully. His eyes set on a point and he became rigid. Far down the slope he could see the two trackers; they were little more than dots or scurrying ants and behind them a larger ant.

Juana had turned to look at him and she saw his back stiffen.

'How far?' she asked quietly.

'They will be here by evening,' said Kino. He looked up the long steep chimney of the cleft where the water came down. 'We must go west,' he said, and his eyes searched the stone shoulder behind the cleft. And thirty feet up on the grey shoulder he saw a series of little erosion caves. He slipped off his sandals and clambered up to them, gripping the bare stone with his toes, and he looked into the shallow caves. They were only a few feet deep, wind-hollowed scoops, but they sloped slightly downwards and back Kino crawled into the largest one and lay down and knew that he could not be seen from the outside. Quickly he went back to Juana.

'You must go up there. Perhaps they will not find us there,' he said.

Without question she filled her water-bottle to the top, and then Kino helped her up to the shallow cave and brought up the packages of food and passed them to her. And Juana sat in the cave entrance and watched him. She saw that he did not try to erase their tracks in the sand. Instead, he climbed up the brush cliff beside the water, clawing and tearing at the ferns and wild grape as he went. And when he had climbed a hundred feet to the next bench, he came down again. He looked carefully at the smooth rock shoulder towards the cave to see that there was no trace of passage, and last he climbed up and crept into the cave beside Juana.

'When they go up,' he said, 'we will slip away, down to the lowlands again. I am afraid only that the baby may cry. You must see that he does not cry.'

'He will not cry,' she said, and she raised the baby's face to her own and looked into his eyes and he stared solemnly back at her.

'He knows,' said Juana.

Now Kino lay in the cave entrance, his chin braced on his crossed arms, and he watched the blue shadow of the mountain move out across the brushy desert below until it reached the Gulf, and the long twilight of the shadow was over the land.

The trackers were long in coming, as though they had trouble with the trail Kino had left. It was dusk when they came at last to the little pool. And all three were on foot now, for a horse could not climb the last steep slope. From above they were thin figures in the evening. The two trackers scurried about on the little beach, and they saw Kino's progress up the cliff before they drank. The man with the rifle sat down and rested himself, and the trackers squatted near him, and in the evening the points of their cigarettes glowed and receded. And then Kino could see that they were eating, and the soft murmur of their voices came to him.

Then darkness fell, deep and black in the mountain cleft. The animals that used the pool came near and smelled men there and drifted away again into the darkness.

He heard a murmur behind him. Juana was whispering, 'Coyotito.' She was begging him to be quiet. Kino heard the baby whimper, and he knew from the muffled sounds that Juana had covered his head with her shawl.

Down on the beach a match flared, and in its momentary light Kino saw that two of the men were sleeping, curled up like dogs, while the third watched, and he saw the glint of the rifle in the match light. And then the match died, but it left a picture on Kino's eyes. He could see it, just how each man was, two sleeping curled up and the third squatting in the sand with the rifle between his knees.

Kino moved silently back into the cave. Juana's eyes were two sparks reflecting a low star. Kino crawled quietly close to her and he put his lips near to her cheek.

'There is a way,' he said.

'But they will kill you.'

'If I get first to the one with the rifle,' Kino said, 'I must get to him first, then I will be all right. Two are sleeping.'

Her hand crept out from under her shawl and gripped his arm. 'They will see your white clothes in the starlight.'

'No,' he said. 'And I must go before moonrise.'

He searched for a soft word and then gave it up. 'If they kill me,' he said, 'lie quietly. And when they are gone away, go to Loreto.'

Her hand shook a little, holding his wrist.

'There is no choice,' he said. 'It is the only way. They will find us in the morning.'

Her voice trembled a little. 'Go with God,' she said.

He peered closely at her and he could see her large eyes. Her hand fumbled out and found the baby, and for a moment his palm lay on Coyotito's head. And then Kino raised his hand and touched Juana's cheek, and she held her breath.

Against the sky in the cave entrance Juana could see that Kino was taking off his white clothes, for dirty and ragged though they were they would show up against the dark night. His own brown skin was a better protection for him. And then she saw how he hooked his amulet neck-string about the horn handle of his great knife, so that it hung down in front of him and left both hands free. He did not come back to her. For a moment his body was black in the cave entrance, crouched and silent, and then he was gone.

111

Juana moved to the entrance and looked out. She peered like an owl from the hole in the mountain, and the baby slept under the blanket on her back, his face turned sideways against her neck and shoulder. She could feel his warm breath against her skin, and Juana whispered her combination of prayer and magic, her Hail Marys and her ancient intercession, against the black unhuman things.

The night seemed a little less dark when she looked out, and to the east there was a lightening in the sky, down near the horizon where the moon would show. And, looking down, she could see the cigarette of the man on watch.

Kino edged like a slow lizard down the smooth rock shoulder. He had turned his neck-string so that the great knife hung down from his back and could not clash against the stone. His spread fingers gripped the mountain, and his bare toes found support through contact, and even his chest lay against the stone so that he would not slip. For any sound, a rolling pebble or a sigh, a little slip of flesh on rock, would rouse the watchers below. Any sound that was not germane to the night would make them alert. But the night was not silent; the little tree frogs that lived near the stream twittered like birds, and the high metallic ringing of the cicadas filled the mountain cleft. And Kino's own music was in his head, the music of the enemy, low and pulsing, nearly asleep. But the Song of the Family had become as fierce and sharp and feline as the snarl of a female puma. The family song was alive now and driving him down on the dark enemy. The harsh cicada seemed to take up its melody, and the twittering tree frogs called little phrases of it.

And Kino crept silently as a shadow down the smooth mountain face. One bare foot moved a few inches and the toes touched the stone and gripped, and the other foot a few inches, and then the palm of one hand a little downwards, and then the other hand, until the whole body, without seeming to move, had moved. Kino's mouth was open so that even his breath would make no sound, for he knew that he was not invisible. If the watcher, sensing movement, looked at the dark place against the stone which was his body, he could see him. Kino must move so slowly he would not draw the watcher's eyes. It took him a long time to reach the bottom and to crouch behind a little dwarf palm. His heart thundered in his chest and his hands and face were wet with sweat. He crouched and took great long breaths to calm himself.

Only twenty feet separated him from the enemy now, and he tried to remember the ground between. Was there any stone which might trip him in his rush? He kneaded his legs against cramp and found that his muscles were jerking after their long tension. And then he looked apprehensively to the east. The moon would rise in a few moments now, and he must attack before it rose. He could see the outline of the watcher, but the sleeping men were below his vision. It was the watcher Kino must find must find quickly and without hesitation. Silently he drew the amulet string over his shoulder and loosened the loop from the horn-handle of his great knife.

He was too late, for as he rose from his crouch the silver edge of the moon slipped above the eastern horizon, and Kino sank back behind his bush.

It was an old and ragged moon, but it threw hard light and hard shadow into the mountain cleft, and now Kino could see the seated figure of the watcher on the little beach beside the pool. The watcher gazed full at the moon, and then he lighted another cigarette, and the match illumined his dark face for a moment. There could be no waiting now; when the watcher turned his head, Kino must leap. His legs were as tight as wound springs.

And then from above came a little murmuring cry. The watcher turned his head to listen and then he stood up, and one of the sleepers stirred on the ground and awakened and asked quietly, 'What is it?'

'I don't know,' said the watcher. 'It sounded like a cry, almost like a human – like a baby.'

The man who had been sleeping said, 'You can't tell. Some coyote bitch with a litter. I've heard a coyote pup cry like a baby.'

The sweat rolled in drops down Kino's forehead and fell into his eyes and burned them. The little cry came again and the watcher looked up the side of the hill to the dark cave.

'Coyote maybe,' he said, and Kino heard the harsh click as he cocked the rifle.

'If it's a coyote, this will stop it,' the watcher said as he raised the gun.

Kino was in mid-leap when the gun crashed and the barrel-flash made a picture on his eyes. The great knife swung and crunched hollowly. It bit through neck and deep into chest, and Kino was a terrible machine now. He grasped the rifle even as he wrenched free his knife. His strength and his movement and his speed were a machine. He whirled and struck the head of the seated an like a melon. The third man scrabbled away like a crab, slipped into the pool, and then he began to climb frantically, to climb up the cliff where the water pencilled down. His hands and feet threshed in the tangle of the wild grapevine, and he whimpered and gibbered as he tried to get up. But Kino had become as cold and deadly as steel. Deliberately he threw the lever of the rifle, and then he raised the gun and aimed deliberately and fired. He saw his enemy tumble backwards into the pool, and Kino strode to the water. In the moonlight he could see the frantic frightened eyes, and Kino aimed and fired between the eyes.

And then Kino stood uncertainly. Something was wrong, some signal was trying to get through to his brain. Tree frogs and cicadas were silent now. And then Kino's brain cleared from its red concentration and he knew the sound – the keening, moaning, rising hysterical cry from the little cave in the side of the stone mountain, the cry of death.

Everyone in La Paz remembers the return of the family; there may be some old ones who saw it, but those whose fathers and whose grandfathers told it to them remember it nevertheless. It is an event that happened to everyone.

It was late in the golden afternoon when the first little boys ran hysterically into the town and spread the word that Kino and Juana were coming back. And everyone hurried to see them. The sun was settling towards the western mountains and the shadows on the ground were long. And perhaps that was what left the deep impression on those who saw them.

The two came from the rutted country road into the city, and they were not walking in single file, Kino ahead and Juana behind, as usual, but side by side. The sun was behind them and their long shadows stalked ahead, and they seemed to carry two towers of darkness with them. Kino had a rifle across his arm and Juana carried her shawl like a sack over her shoulder. And in it was a small, limp, heavy bundle. The shawl was crusted with dried blood, and the bundle swayed a little as she walked. Her face was hard and lined and leathery with fatigue and with the tightness with which she fought fatigue. And her wide eyes stared inwards on herself. She was as remote and as removed as Heaven. Kino's lips were thin and his jaws tight, and the people say that he carried fear with him, that he was as dangerous as a rising storm. The people say that the two seemed to be removed from human experience; that they had gone through pain and had come out on the other side; that there was almost a

116

magical protection about them. And those people who had rushed to see them crowded back and let them pass and did not speak to them.

Kino and Juana walked through the city as though it were not there. Their eyes glanced neither right nor left nor up nor down, but stared only straight ahead. Their legs moved a little jerkily, like well-made wooden dolls, and they carried pillars of black fear about them. And, as they walked through the stone and plaster city, brokers peered at them from barred windows and servants put one eye to a slitted gate and mothers turned the faces of their youngest children inwards against their skirts; Kino and Juana strode side by side through the stone and plaster city and down among the brush houses, and the neighbours stood back and let them pass. Juan Tomás raised his hand in greeting and did not say the greeting and left his hand in the air for a moment uncertainly.

In Kino's ears the Song of the Family was as fierce as a cry. He was immune and terrible, and his song had become a battle cry. They trudged past the burned square where their house had been without even looking at it. They cleared the brush that edged the beach and picked their way down the shore towards the water. And they did not look towards Kino's broken canoe.

And when they came to the water's edge they stopped and stared out over the Gulf. And then Kino laid the rifle down, and he dug among his clothes, and then he held the great pearl in his hand. He looked into its surface and it was grey and ulcerous. Evil faces peered from it into his eyes, and he saw the light of burning. And in the surface of the pearl he saw the frantic eyes of the man in the pool. And in the surface of the pearl he saw Coyotito lying in the little cave with the top of his head shot away. And the pearl was ugly; it was grey, like a malignant growth. And Kino heard the music of the pearl, distorted and insane. Kino's hand shook a little, and he turned slowly to Juana and held the pearl out to her. She stood beside him, still holding her dead bundle over her shoulder. She looked at the pearl in his hand for a moment and then she looked into Kino's eyes and said softly, 'No, you.'

And Kino drew back his arm and flung the pearl with all his might. Kino and Juana watched it go, winking and glimmering under the setting sun. They saw the little splash in the distance, and they stood side by side watching the place for a long time.

And the pearl settled into the lovely green water and dropped towards the bottom. The waving branches of the algæ called to it and beckoned to it. The lights on its surface were green and lovely. It settled down to the sand bottom among the fern-like plants. Above, the surface of the water was a green mirror. And the pearl lay on the floor of the sea. A crab scampering over the bottom raised a little cloud of sand, and when it settled the pearl was gone.

And the music of the pearl drifted to a whisper and disappeared.

Further reading

Other books by John Steinbeck

If you have enjoyed reading *The Pearl*, you might want to read some other books by John Steinbeck. (Your local library will have copies of these.)

The Long Valley (1938) is a collection of several stories, including 'The Red Pony' about farming in the Salinas valley.

Cup of Gold (1929) is a novel based on the life of the pirate, Sir Henry Morgan.

Of Mice and Men (1937) tells the powerful story of George and Lennie who are itinerant farm workers with a dream.

The Moon is Down (1942) in which a northern European town is taken over by brutal invaders, but gradually the townspeople learn to fight back. Based on the German invasion of Norway in the Second World War.

Cannery Row (1945) is a hilarious story of life in a semi-derelict fish-canning town.

The Short Reign of Pippin IV (1957) in which in desperation, the wrangling politicians of France decide to restore the monarchy.

Works by other authors

Animal Farm by George Orwell (1945) in which the animals of Manor Farm decide to evict the farmer and run the farm themselves with unexpected consequences. An allegorical story based on the Bolshevik revolution in Russia.

'The Bottle Imp' by R.L. Stevenson (1893) the story of how a magical bottle brings evil to its owners.

'The Monkey's Paw' by W.W. Jacobs (1898) in which the dried paw of a dead monkey can grant three wishes, but the way these wishes are granted only causes misery.

The Pardoner's Tale by Geoffrey Chaucer (1387–1400) in which three hooligans find a cache of gold coins and in their greed manage to destroy each other.

These last two stories can both be found in Twisters, published by Longman (2000).

Programme of study

1. Write a description of Kino's hut, saying what it is made of and how it is furnished. How does the hut differ from the doctor's house in the town?

2. Write an imaginary conversation between Kino's elder brother, Juan Tomás, and his wife Apolonia when they first hear of Kino's marvellous discovery. Do not forget to show in this conversation that you understand what these two characters are like and how their views differ from those of Kino and Juana.

3. What mistakes do you think Kino made in his attempts to make his fortune out of the Pearl of the World? If you had been Juan Tomás what advice might you have given Kino to help him achieve his ambitions?

4. How did the villagers try to avoid selling their pearls to the buyers in the town and why did their attempts fail? Could they have tried another way to make sure they were paid a fair price for their wares?

5. What are the differences between Kino's people and the inhabitants of the stone and plaster houses in the town where the doctor lives?

6. Imagine that many years after the events told in the story, a stranger arrives in the native village and wants to hear the story from the point of view of Juan Tomás. Write an account of this meeting, using your knowledge of *The Pearl* to create the atmosphere of the village. For example, Juan Tomás might call on his wife, Apolonia, to bring refreshments, or to verify

a point in the tale. Write as if you were Juan Tomás speaking – that is, without any descriptive passages, but entirely in direct speech. You could start your story with the words, 'I myself saw it happen ...'

7. 'If this story is a parable, perhaps everyone takes his own meaning from it and reads his own life into it.' What do you understand by the term *parable*? What elements of a parable are there in *The Pearl*? Why do you think Steinbeck chose to write his story as a parable? In your answer you may wish to refer to other examples of parables which you have read, and compare their narrative styles with that of *The Pearl*.

8. Steinbeck first heard the tale of the Pearl of the World when on a marine collecting trip in the Gulf of California. Many of the descriptions of nature in *The Pearl* are concerned with life near and in water. Look again at these descriptive passages and explain why, in your opinion, Steinbeck chose to place them where they are in the story, and what effect he intended them to have on the reader.

9. Nature and natural objects are often used symbolically in *The Pearl*. For example, the poison of the scorpion's sting has a parallel in the description of the town as a living thing (Chapter 3). Look for other examples of symbolism in *The Pearl*, and say what you think the symbols represent and what effect they are intended to have on the reader.

10. In the village community where Kino and Juana live, what might a husband's expectations be of his wife? How well does Juana live up to Kino's expectations of her? How does her attitude to Kino and his expectations of her change during the story? At what stages in the story do these changes occur? Why do you think these changes come about? What is the

relationship between them at the end of the story? How do we know this?

11. What changes do you think would have to be made to the novel *The Pearl* to make it suitable for making into a film? Before you start your answer, think about the main differences between a film and a book, taking into account amongst other things
   - how the story line might be conveyed to a film audience
   - how to suggest the historical background to the story
   - the presentation of the descriptive passages
   - how to convey character
   - the use of music and other effects.

12. Write brief pen-portraits of three of the following characters from *The Pearl*: Kino; Juana; the doctor; Juan Tomás; the stout pearl buyer; the priest.

   Amongst other things you could include in your descriptions references to the characters' appearance (including mannerisms of speech or walking), behaviour, hopes and ambitions, attitudes to others and what others think of them. To each pen-portrait add your opinion of the character you are describing.

13. What evidence can you find in *The Pearl* that the Spanish Mexicans considered the native villagers to be primitive and to be ignored as far as possible? How does this attitude handicap Kino in his attempts to better himself and his family, and how does it help him to survive?

14. Steinbeck wrote in a letter to a friend: 'It seems that two forces are necessary in a man before he is a man.' These forces – of good and of evil – are present in Kino. How do

they show themselves in his behaviour and how does he struggle to overcome the evil. When he says to Juana, 'I am a man' (page 84), what do you understand Steinbeck to have meant when he put these words into Kino's mouth?

Glossary

The meaning of the words and phrases given here are suited to this text only. They may have other meanings elsewhere.

17	**roosters:** cockerels
	tuna: prickly pear
18	**dank:** unpleasantly damp
19	**frantically:** with wild frenzy
	interval: difference of pitch between notes
20	**feinted:** made mock attacks
	game chickens: chickens bred for fighting
	pulque: fermented drink made of agave juice
21	**scorpion:** member of the spider family with crab-like claws and a stinging tail
	plaintively: mournfully
	Hail Mary: prayer used by Roman Catholics
22	**lymphatic:** fluid filled
24	**strenuous:** vigorous
	bougainvillaea: tropical climbing plant with brilliant flowers
	plaza: town square
25	**appraised:** assess
	scandal: malicious gossip
	avarice: greed
	abortions: ending of pregnancies
	alms: charitable gift
	indigent: in need (but Steinbeck probably meant indigene)
26	**indigene:** native born
27	**watered silk:** shiny silken cloth with the appearance of having water on it

masses: central religious services of the Roman Catholic Church

subsequent: following

28   **veterinary:** vet

29   **suppliant:** begging (Steinbeck probably meant supplicant)

31   **estuary:** mouth of a river

lateen: triangular

rubble: loose stones, stony

algae: microscopic green plants, seaweed

fiddler crabs: crabs with one claw much enlarged

mirage: image of distant landscape distorted through intense heat

32   **optical:** of the eyes

mangroves: trees which can grow in salt marsh

vibrated: wavered

guarantee: promise

bulwark: fortification

33   **poultice:** healing bandage

unsubstantial: lacking solidity

34   **barnacles:** small shelled sea animal which attaches itself to underwater surfaces

35   **perceptible:** detectable

37   **flutes:** long grooves

illusion: deceptions

incandescence: bright glow

41   **colonial:** like a colony or group

judicious: seeming to have sound judgment

42   **semblance:** appearance

43   **capital:** stock of money

residue: remaining substance

precipitated: formed out of a solution

speculations: imaginative plans

lusts: passionate desires

distillate: concentrated element
outward sea: Pacific Ocean
44 **lucent:** light-giving
45 **harpoon:** fishing spear
carbine: light rifle
disparagement: sneering
46 **prophecy:** mystical prediction
transfigured: changed in appearance
47 **the Father:** the Roman Catholic priest
benediction: blessing
49 **crickets:** insects like grasshoppers
threshed: wagged its tail violently
visualised: seen in the mind's eye
consequently: as a result
50 **subjugation:** being dominated
52 **pitcher:** earthenware jug
53 **aired:** tried out
dissembling: concealing his true intentions
school (of fish): shoal
54 **spasm:** sudden tightening
58 **furtive:** secretive and sly
inaudible: beyond hearing
59 **consecrated:** dedicated to God
60 **tempo:** speed
cozened: betrayed
61 **diffused:** spread out, filtered
63 **tithe:** tenth part share
64 **countenanced:** tolerated
swaddled: wrapped tightly like a newborn baby
66 **waist:** woman's blouse or bodice
self-consciousness: embarrassment
67 **freshet:** stream which appears in wet weather
68 **ramparts:** outer defensive walls of a castle
strangers: Spanish invaders

retirement: retreat from confrontation
69 **saloons:** public bars
benign: kindly
ceremonious: elaborate
70 **hibiscus:** tropical flowering shrub
legerdemain: sleight of hand, conjuring tricks
71 **contemptuous:** sneering
72 **pesos:** Mexican coinage
collusion: conspiracy
73 **coagulating:** thickening
76 **tules:** bullrushes
77 **structure:** form, shape
lethargy: drowsiness, torpor
participation: joining in
78 **kelp:** seaweed
entranced: dazed
87 **conceived:** thought
curdled: solidified
88 **exhilaration:** excitement
89 **lament:** cry or song of woe
90 **leprosy:** much feared skin disease
96 **covert:** thicket
97 **resinous:** smell of the sap of certain trees
99 **sentinel:** sentry, watcher
guttural: throaty
symbolic fighting: the motions of fighting
102 **goading:** nagging
103 **granite:** very hard rock
erosion: wearing away
monolithic: single standing rock, like a monument
pivoting: turning mechanically
105 **irresolution:** indecision
106 **rupture:** split
escarpment: ledge

Title list

Post-1914 Plays

0 582 30242 0	Absent Friends	Alan Ayckbourn
0 582 06019 2	The Winslow Boy	Terrence Rattigan
0 582 22389 X	P'Tang, Yang, Kipperbang & other TV plays	Jack Rosenthal
0 582 43445 9	Educating Rita	Willy Russell
0 582 08173 4	Shirley Valentine	Willy Russell
0 582 25383 7	Ten Short Plays	
0 582 25394 2	Scenes from Plays	
0 582 06014 1	The Royal Hunt of the Sun	Peter Shaffer
0 582 09712 6	Equus	Peter Shaffer
0 582 06015 X	Pygmalion	Bernard Shaw
0 582 07786 9	Saint Joan	Bernard Shaw
0 582 25396 9	The Rivals/The School for Scandal	Richard Brinsley Sheridan

Post-1914 Stories from other Cultures

0 582 28730 8	Quartet of Stories	
0 582 06011 7	July's People	Nadine Gordimer
0 582 25398 5	Heat and Dust	Ruth Prawer Jhabvala
0 582 07787 7	Cry, the Beloved Country	Alan Paton
0 582 03922 3	Stories from Asia	
0 582 25393 4	Stories from Africa	
0 582 28929 7	Global Tales	

Post-1914 Non-Fiction

0 582 25391 8	Genres
0 582 25384 5	Diaries and Letters
0 582 28932 7	Introducing Media
0 582 25386 1	Travel Writing
0 582 08837 2	Autobiographies
0 582 01736 X	The Diary of Anne Frank

Pre-1914 Fiction

0 582 07720 6	Pride and Prejudice	Jane Austen
0 582 07719 2	Jane Eyre	Charlotte Brontë
0 582 07782 6	Wuthering Heights	Emily Brontë
0 582 07783 4	Great Expectations	Charles Dickens
0 582 28729 4	Oliver Twist	Charles Dickens
0 582 23664 9	A Christmas Carol	Charles Dickens
0 582 23662 2	Silas Marner	George Eliot
0 582 22586 8	The Mayor of Casterbridge	Thomas Hardy
0 582 07788 5	Far from the Madding Crowd	Thomas Hardy
0 582 30244 7	Ethan Frome	Edith Wharton

Pre-1914 Collections

0 582 25405 1	Wessex Tales	Thomas Hardy
0 582 28931 9	Stories Old and New	
0 582 28927 0	War Stories	
0 582 25388 8	Characters from Pre-20th Century Novels	
0 582 25384 5	Diaries and Letters	
0 582 25385 3	Highlights from 19th Century Novels	
0 582 25389 6	Landmarks	
0 582 25386 1	Travel Writing	
0 582 33807 7	19th Century Short Stories of Passion & Mystery	

Pre-1914 Poetry

0 582 22585 X	Poems from Other Centuries

Pre-1914 Plays

0 582 25397 7	She Stoops to Conquer	Oliver Goldsmith
0 582 24948 1	Three Plays	Henrik Ibsen
0 582 25409 4	Doctor Faustus	Christopher Marlowe
0 582 28930 0	Starting Shakespeare	
0 582 43444 0	The Devil's Disciple	Bernard Shaw
0 582 07785 0	Arms and the Man	Bernard Shaw
0 582 28731 6	The Duchess of Malfi	John Webster
0 582 07784 2	The Importance of Being Earnest	Oscar Wilde

NEW CENTURY READERS

Post-1914 Contemporary Fiction

0 582 32847 0	Granny the Pag	Nina Bawden
0 582 29254 9	The Real Plato Jones	Nina Bawden
0 582 25395 0	A Question of Courage	Marjorie Darke
0 582 32845 4	Daughter of the Sea	Berlie Doherty
0 582 43455 6	The Snake Stone	Berlie Doherty
0 582 29262 X	My Family and other Natural Disasters	Josephine Feeney
0 582 31941 2	The Tulip Touch	Anne Fine
0 582 43452 1	Flour Babies	Anne Fine
0 582 29257 3	A Pack of Liars	Anne Fine
0 582 29258 1	The Book of the Banshee	Anne Fine
0 582 29261 1	Madame Doubtfire	Anne Fine
0 582 29251 4	Step by Wicked Step	Anne Fine
0 582 29260 3	Goggle Eyes	Anne Fine
0 582 29255 7	MapHead	Lesley Howarth

0 582 43453 X	A Northern Childhood	George Layton
0 582 32846 2	Lizzie's Leaving	Joan Lingard
0 582 31967 6	Night Fires	Joan Lingard
0 582 43456 4	Goodnight Mister Tom	Michelle Magorian
0 582 43451 3	Journey to Jo'burg	Beverley Naidoo
0 582 36419 1	Aquila	Andrew Norriss
0 582 29256 5	Along a Lonely Road	Catherine Sefton
0 582 46148 0	The Red Pony	John Steinbeck
0 582 31966 8	A Serpent's Tooth	Robert Swindells
0 582 31968 4	Follow a Shadow	Robert Swindells
0 582 31964 1	Urn Burial	Robert Westall

Post-1914 Poetry

| 0 582 25400 0 | Poems 1 |
| 0 582 22587 6 | Poems in my Earphone |

Post-1914 Plays

0 582 43450 5	Mirad, a Boy from Bosnia	Ad de Bont
0 582 09556 5	Bill's New Frock	Anne Fine
0 582 09555 7	Collision Course	Nigel Hinton
0 582 09554 9	Maid Marian and her Merry Men	Tony Robinson
0 582 10156 5	The Fwog Prince	Kaye Umansky

Pre-1914

| 0 582 42944 7 | Oliver Twist | Charles Dickens |
| 0 582 29253 0 | Twisters |